I0675278

SOUL SAVER
By
Margaret Afseth

ISBN: 978-1-927828-49-6

Publisher's note: This novel is a work of fiction. Names, characters, places and incidents are either products of the author's imagination or used fictitiously. All characters are fictional, and similarity to people living or dead purely coincidental.

This book is dedicated to all those women exploited, abandoned, and abused in our world.

Table of Contents

PROLOGUE:

Ice at the water's edge; steam clouds rising in the air; the gurgle of a gently rushing watercourse just out of sight. Trees covered in hoarfrost above; dark obscuring everything.

Liam crouched in the bushes with the young ones, waiting near the river bank, until it should be safe. In this disguise, it felt cold, damp, uncomfortable. Static made the fur of his body tingle.

The water nearby filled him with dread, but this was where he'd found the young kits hiding. It was dangerous here; the youngsters could fall in; the humans had a weapon to drown the pair, and if the Roog came along, they too might use it to their advantage. Thankfully, the dogs preferred to stick to land.

This human world had always seemed hazardous at best, and this time it was more so; they had much too long to wait before he could give the signal for pick up. The shuttle was caught beyond the solar system, concealed, cloaked, avoiding a Roog battleship.

"This spot is not secure; we need to get beyond the buildings," Liam decided. "Darkness might hide the smaller primitive cat, but not those of us who are larger."

"Where should we go, poppa?" asked the five year old male.

Liam gestured toward a path above, and they ascended the bank together quickly. Once up there, the way led along the embankment, through an illuminated park that was adequately treed. But the light made the elder male uneasy, wary, cautious, yet he had little choice but to take this route.

"Poppa..." the female complained. "I am cold."

"I know, little she. When we are at a safer location, I will build you a fire."

5

In his lifetime, Liam had saved many across the universe. When he found them, they were most often alone, their parents killed by Roog, or captured, which was as good as a death sentence in itself. And though the parents had hidden and sacrificed for them, setting out the beacon for rescue, by the time Liam got to them, the little beings were foraging to survive, in bins of garbage behind the businesses. Upon his arrival in their hostile environment, he became their lone protector, and this fact alone bonded the little ones to him.

Because of his age, many of the children called him Poppa, a nick name implying grandfather in his culture. Liam cherished this designation!

Always, when bringing them in, he made certain they were adopted by a new family, and kept in touch, returning often for visits. Because of this, wherever he went he had a welcome, and was called Poppa by the younger generation. It was the closest he could come to having children of his own.

And this had been how he had staffed his momma Dia's med ship. He had once been a lost kit himself, alone, different. Dia had taken him in, accepted his unusual character and parentage.

****

Liam heard the crashing, blinded, panicked escape of the person fleeing toward them before the creature stumbled into sight. When the human woman broke into the path directly ahead of them, the left side of her face next to her eye, and down the cheek, was covered in dry blood. She was limping, gasping with exhaustion, running erratically, eyes closed, arms outstretched before her, feeling her way along.

Suddenly, she caught her foot on an exposed root; went sprawling, right into Liam's arms. He reached out to catch her just before her knees found the leafy peat beneath their feet.

"Help me," she pleaded, in a voice that was soft and raspy, weak from fatigue. "They found me."

She must think I'm someone she knows.

At their touch, due to his empathic ability, Liam became aware of two things: first, she was trembling with unreasoning terror; and second, she'd been drugged excessively, and the preparation was just beginning to effect her. She went limp against him, going senseless.

Liam sniffed at the air.

Danger is coming! I can smell the obnoxious odor of Roog.

It's time to leave the path!

"Hide, little ones!" he growled urgently in the Feline tongue. "Under the bushes. Quickly! Our enemy approaches!"

Lifting the unconscious female, he rapidly followed his charges, to dive and burrow with them deep beneath the foliage.

Their escape was none too soon.

Liam held his breath as the giant hunters loped by, moving upright; as always, unaware and unperceptive, expecting their quarry to be far ahead, and not beneath their feet. Large, with unconcealed dog-like heads, their bodies were camouflaged in human garments.

Liam was intimately familiar with masquerade practices. It was a strategy used by both Roog and Feline. Whether on the hunt or fleeing, each wore a camouflage belt, which could change the outward perception of their visible image. His father's race used it to protect themselves, whereas the Roog employed it mostly to confuse their prey.

The colossal dog creatures hunted humans as food. And just as easily, would kill or torture any of Liam's kind, just for the sport of it. It was their favorite pastime to seek the weaker young, and especially all females. No life was sacred or safe from them.

It is unusual though for them to wear only half disguise. I wonder why they've become so brave?

The young kits beside him flinched, as the pack passed over them. The female gave a hissing moan. Liam stroked her fur, and cautioned.

"Shush, little she. They will hear."

Liam knew their cover was good, the bushes large and full.

The male twin worriedly added his challenge.

"They will scent us, Poppa?" he whispered fearfully. "They can find us?"

His tone said much, revealing just beneath the surface, the memory of the last encounter, in which they'd lost their parents to these beasts of prey. The grief was poignant.

"If I can help it; they'll not have you," Liam disagreed in a low growl.

The woman beneath him stirred. Roughly, to silence any sound, he placed his hand across her mouth, clutching her tightly in his arms. Her reaction was to struggle against his hold.

"Be still!" Liam hissed in human English. "I am not your enemy. They will hear you."

She went quiet in compliance, easing into his shoulder.

On high alert, Liam listened as the diminishing sounds faded. The fog was descending around them, but he knew it would not really hide them. Their dark bodies would soon stand out, visible shadows against the white.

And the Roog would turn around when they realized they had lost the trail.

When Liam was certain the enemy was out of range, he risked speaking again.

"Come children. We must keep moving."

He rose, easily lifting the human with him. Still carrying her, he proceeded along the path away from the threat of danger. For safety, he kept her lips covered with the palm of his hand, just to make certain she did not cry out.

A moment later, the female made a weak attempt to pull away his hand. Liam stopped, knowing she wished to communicate.

"Will you promise not to cry out if I remove my hand?" At her nod, he loosed his hold, and added, "I am Liam. I will see that you are tended to."

Though in an obvious drugged state, she wanted to be let down. Rather than argue, he let her try to stand. Her legs buckled, so he scooped her up again, and took off at a rapid pace, the young ones loping after to keep up with him. He stopped to rest only when the little female began to lag. By then, his burden was once more in oblivion.

He knelt with the human on his knee, giving the young ones the break they so desperately needed. Looking about him, Liam noticed the end of the park was just ahead.

As he rested, he took note of the woman he carried. He reproached himself for taking on this unnecessary challenge.

Why am I taking her with us, anyway? I could just leave her in the entrance of a building, where her own kind would find her, and give her medical treatment. It would certainly be easier on the kits.

Yet he feared, if she wasn't found immediately, the delay might cost her life.

Liam shook his head, frustrated at his dilemma.

He examined the wound next to her eye.

That was inflicted by a taser!

Raw and still bleeding, the damage seemed to be more inside than exterior.

Her eyes must sting and burn when she tries to open them. Her head is throbbing constantly, yet she's not uttered a word of complaint, as if she's used to constant pain.

Odd.

Perhaps, it's a blessing she cannot see; that way she'll not realize we are not of her race.

He passed his hand across her forehead attempting to ease the pain the poor women was experiencing. In shock, Liam unexpectedly connected with her inner mind.

Recent and some past memories flashed by in an instant; among them, a vivid recall of a scarred and ancient appearing female. In that spilt second, Liam became aware the one he was viewing was half Noor as he was. He also watched as the she Noor used her powers in a vain attempt to rescue a third woman, and realized that the one he held in his arms, had somehow been responsible for the situation.

At this recollection, a hatred of such intensity, focused on this elder, emanated menacingly from his charge. Liam pulled away in disgusted outrage. He studied the face before him.

Am I harboring an enemy; someone dangerous to me?

Rebuking himself, he shook away the thought.

No! I cannot be a judge. I am a healer; rescuer. I do not have all the facts.

He put the memory away, and went to other things he had seen.

A more recent experience was the one in which the human had encountered the Roog. Two had surprised her, the first, coming from behind, had tasered her, while the second had shot a drug into her opposite shoulder. She had jerked away involuntarily, before the complete dose had been administered.

Liam sat thinking; he grew hopeful.

She may not have gotten enough to kill her, after all.

He noted a distinct change in her breathing.

She's awake again.

"Do you know where you are female?" Liam asked. "Who am I?"

"Liam," she answered groggily.

"Do you have a name?"

"Lana."

"And...how did you escape from the Roog, Lana?"

"I...I played dead. It always works. When they turned away, I ran."

Liam frowned.

First off, she didn't ask what a Roog was; she already knew. That alone proves she has had experience with them before. For such a one, they won't stop looking. And that is decidedly bad for those with her.

The young male kit tugged at Liam's elbow, mewling in fear.

"Poppa, we are afraid..."

His responsibility thundered to the forefront. He'd completely forgotten his charges.

Ah, yes. Young Felines, when stressed, are especially sensitive to my mood changes. I assumed I wouldn't need to cloak.

And they feel exposed out here.

What's wrong with you, Liam? You addlebrained dimwit.

"Sorry," he murmured contritely. "Forgive Poppa, little ones. I got distracted."

Shifting the woman, Liam stood to his feet, and looked about him. "We need to find a place to shelter." Then he added in human, for the sole benefit of the woman in his arms. "Do you know...is there a building nearby where we can find medical attention?"

She was confused, her head lolling against his chest, too heavy to hold up. "Homeless...shelter," she uttered with difficulty. "Take...the street...going west."

Can I trust her word?

Liam panned the view beyond the park, and saw, just ahead, the street in question.

"They...are having...a holiday..." Lana sighed heavily, fighting the drowsiness. Her words slurred. "Should...be open...though."

Holiday?

It was then Liam noticed, in the distance, small children in costume: ghosts and goblins, witches, and some, only in monster masks. Each one carried a small bucket or cloth sack.

I've read of this practice from their histories. The festival is called Halloween. The children are given treats when they beg at the doors of the houses.

No wonder the Roog dare to walk undisguised on the surface this night!

"Stay close, little ones," Liam ordered, taking off down the fog filled street. "I will keep the pace slow, but we cannot stop to rest again. Keep in the shadows, so we are not noticed."

Lana had once again drifted off into her drugged sleep.

Five blocks later, just when Liam was beginning to wonder just how far away this shelter was, and if maybe he had missed it, the woman rallied again.

"Put me down," Lana pleaded, struggling weakly against him. "I can walk..."

She'll slow us down. Oh how I wish I'd not taken this on. Just being with her is dangerous. If she's tagged, the dogs are following. I just want this over with!

But the weight of her was getting too much to carry, and Liam needed to relax his muscles. Rather than argue, he slowed, shifted Lana to her feet, and supporting still, his arm around her, they gradually proceeded.

Lana made it just one block, when her limbs gave way beneath. It had been just enough reprieve to give Liam new energy. He caught her up again, and she sank against his shoulder gratefully.

"Why can't I see?" she quietly whispered, as they went on.

"They blinded you with a taser blast, hoping you couldn't run."

She laughed, and the sound was filled with spite and premeditated malice.

"Fooled them, didn't I?"

He did not smile at that. He knew for certain then, she would mean him harm, as well, if she discovered what he was.

Oh, yes, little she. You are a smart one. I'd best be careful in my dealings with you.

Thankfully, Lana passed out again.

****

Just ahead Liam caught sight of humans blocking their way. There was nowhere to go but through them, not with Lana in his arms.

How much farther is it?

Liam made a quick decision.

From birth every kit was taught to use a camouflage belt. He'd equipped the young ones immediately upon arrival. Liam dropped into the lower Feline tongue the primitives used.

This was a language used mostly in battle, more sounds, hisses and growls, than actual words.

Liam warned, "We approach man. Go human, and stay that way until I tell you otherwise."

The small pair obeyed him without question. Each depressed the middle buckle on their belt, and shifted shape.

Liam, being Noor, a Mental with powers beyond any known others, able to manipulate material, and a shape-shifter, as well, needed no belt.

From a man-size Feline, Liam became a humanoid; his tail vanished; the tiny cat ears slipped beneath his hair; the eyes changed; the nose elongated. No longer was he covered in soft short fur; jeans, a bulky sweater, and a shiny, brown leather jacket replaced that covering. Pliable matching mukluks covered the once paw-like feet.

Beside him, the kits became identical twins, a boy and a girl, with short wavy black hair and tanned brownish skin. Each was dressed similarly to Liam.

Now, the group appeared to be just a father walking home with his children...carrying momma in his arms.

Liam hoped it would be enough to protect them.

****

Until this moment the darkness had shielded them, but presently they were coming up on a street lamp that would illuminate them fully.

Just ahead, a prostitute leaned into the open window of a car talking with the lone front seat occupant inside. Like a wild primitive in heat, her rear was raised, one high-heeled, booted foot moving back and forth, like a flicking tail. With her short skirt and fishnet stockings, it was clear she wore no undergarment.

Humans are such perverts! They have such a perchance for immorality.

The young ones do not need to see this!

Liam felt the children shudder, as they came abreast of another pair of women, standing in the lamp light, as seductively attired as the first. He realized, their reaction was not fear, but revulsion, as they read body language that was considered depraved in their culture.

To comfort, Liam spoke softly under his breath. "Little ones, pay them no mind."

But what was meant to ease, turned the eyes of another, standing back in the shadows, toward them. Liam had failed to notice until too late, because his mind was focused on the backseat passengers he'd just noticed in the car.

This new human was male, dressed all in black clothing. He had blended way too well with the darkness. Now, as he moved toward them threateningly, Liam almost hissed with the abruptness of the shock, before he caught himself.

"Well now," the human challenged as he came out of hiding. "Just what do we have here?" He laughed contemptuously. "Shouldn't keep your drunken bitch up so late." He grinned lecherously. "If she weren't so ugly, I could put her to work."

His manner changed abruptly. "Maybe, you got some money on you, eh? How about handing it over, bud?"

Liam's timid, non confrontational Feline nature took the upper hand. "We have no currency. Honest." he declared truthfully.

The man eyed him with suspicion for long moments, decided there was truth in the statement, then suddenly, he caught sight of the young children peeking out from behind Liam's back.

Liam slipped into the man's mind, watching the lustful hunger flood over him, as he spied the young girl. He cringed, and shivered visibly.

"Now, your kid," the human observed solicitously. "She's just ripe. She'd be worth a lot to me. I have guys lined up, who'd pay plenty for her."

The man spoke directly to the five year old. "What say, honey? Would you like some candy? Come with me, and I'll always take care of you. Leave your old man, and come live off the rich. I promise it'll be worth your while."

It was a good thing the little she was so very terrified; if she had hissed at him the way she wanted to, their cover would have been blown.

Am I going to have to use my powers to protect, after all? Even here a young female is prey!

But the man was abruptly pushing passed them, seeing danger to the girls he already had. An unmarked police car had slowly approached, and those inside were accessing the situation on the sidewalk.

"Get out of here," tersely growled the pimp, motioning toward a side street escape route. "I'll catch up to you later."

Liam didn't need to be told a second time. He fled into the night, his strides long and rapid; the best he could do without actually running. His little charges did have to scurry to keep up.

Behind them, the policemen were too intent on the women and their handler, to challenge Liam and his entourage.

Minutes later, they came out on another street, and came upon the entrance of an emergency clinic. Liam breathed a sigh of relief. With the hope she'd be found shortly, and tended to, he placed his burden just inside the doors, then stepped outside again.

With the two disguised kits in his arms, he teleported to the edge of the city, where he quickly found an old abandoned barn in which to spend the night safely.

Chapter 1

Feather was named by her Caucasian father.

His idea of native culture had been derived from movies and the news: episodes of knife fights, robberies, and murders done by drunken, misplaced aboriginals back in his home city on the prairies. He knew nothing of the Haida, or the Raven clan of British Columbia, to which her mother had belonged.

He decided Feather was a name that would honor the woman who had died at her birth.

Her second name came to him when he viewed the tiny premature infant. She had barely fit into the palm of his hand. And even now, at twenty-eight, Feather Cloud was small and lean, only five foot tall and ninety-five pounds.

Father had been a transplant to Vancouver, a man with a love of drink and prostitutes, but he'd taken such a liking to Feather's mother, he persuaded her to shack up permanently, just to get her off the streets. They had only been together a year and a half, when Feather came along, and he lost this chosen companion.

Feather's memory of her first years were hazy. In recollection, two facts stood out: her birth mother was always idolized by her father, but not the peoples from which she stemmed; and...when poppa wanted to party, Feather must be locked in her room.

Then, at the age of five, while driving drunk, her father had plowed his battered pickup into the back of a semi, and was flattened beneath it. Left an orphan, somehow, Feather came into the hands of nuns.

In the orphanage, she was told that she was under a curse, that her mother's lineage was not something to be proud of, but shamed her. If she was to be saved from such predilection, she must work diligently to better herself, forget her debased beginnings, and embrace all that was good in a woman, by keeping free of degenerate men. She must become holy...apart, as those who were rearing her.

And truly, Feather did her utmost to comply, doing her chores: scrubbing floors, working in the kitchens, doing laundry for her keep. But discipline always seemed to find her. If she was slow, her work unsatisfactory...or she was caught in a lie, the young girl was strapped. In the opinion of her caregivers, it was the only form of punishment that conquered her rebellious nature.

It mattered not, that the first time she was disbelieved, she had actually told the truth. It had been another blaming her out of spite.

By this, Feather learn at an early age, an untruth was more believable than fact, and instead of the punishment threatened, actually produced reward. Of course, when her duplicity was discovered, which it often was, it ended in yet another strapping. Many a night, she moaned over hands raw, not from harsh housework, but the welts of a chastisement.

At the age of fifteen, she'd had enough, and ran away to the streets of Vancouver. It was here at last, good fortune shone upon her. While in a mall, begging for small change, Feather met an older girl from the Haida nation. As they became friends, comparing backgrounds, and tracing their mother's ancestry, the two discovered they were distant cousins.

And Feather found her people. It was extremely gratifying to finally have roots, and pride in her ancestry; to not be alone anymore, and a part of an intimate supportive system. She had family! Feather found cousins, aunts and uncles... With some she instantly felt a connection, others took time to get to know, and some were offensive or abrasive, as in most regular families, but over all, she felt at home.

She learned her heritage, her belief system: to honor nature, the balance between human, animal, bird, and forest world. Sickness was imbalance, and her greatest desire was to become a Haida healer.

Most of all, Feather enjoyed the Potlatch, for here, at last, her mother was honored among the dead. When the Raven and the Eagle clans met, and the gift giving began, Feather joined her relatives in giving away her treasures, receiving back, from each in turn, new delightful trinkets for future use.

A new lesson was learn now. Possessions were unimportant. They lost their appeal over time, and the value was in relationships, which was what counted in the long run.

****

Feather had spent a day in the city at the mall, just hanging with friends. It was a mild evening, already dark, when she headed back to her battered old Chevy, she had parked in the alley out behind.

She was proud of the fact she was of the Raven clan, her mother's clan, but Raven was a trickster, rebellious and a trouble maker. Free. It was easy for Feather to follow such ways, especially when it came to the rules and laws of the white man; she was not adverse to bending them.

Why should I pay for parking, when the alleyway is free? Besides, my car is just an old beater, anyway. If someone needs it more than I, they can have it.

The lane reeked of many odors: fetid decaying meat, spoiling fruit, and rancid oils. Above that was the stench of urine and fecal matter, enough to make the woman hold her breath, but it was an undisturbed place, safe to hide a vehicle.

As she drew in a quick breath, Feather caught the scent of moisture in the air.

Smells like it's going to rain.

As she passed a rusting green dumpster, a movement in the lighter shadows alerted her, and the low ominous growl of an animal came to her ears. Not often did the scavenging dogs turn and attack; mostly they just slunk away, but just to be safe, Feather picked up from the ground a stick to defend herself. She turned toward the sound.

What she did not expect was the size of the dog. As it rose to full height, it seemed over six feet, towering above her, ferocious as any she had ever encountered. Another thing that did not compute at all, was the fact, it wore shorts.

Man or beast, she wasn't sure, but she raised her arm to cover her face, in a reflex of protection, and with the other hand, attempted to fight for her life.

She never even saw the second beast. The world blinked out abruptly.

Chapter 2

Tusha's first unpleasant discovery had been that a female Noor should never be left by herself. She did not do well without another telepath to balance her. At least, in her experience, she especially, needed the opposition from a male with the same abilities; he was the stabilizer.

And added to that was the additional fact, a Noor alone among humans, who were unable to read or block, was simply inviting torture.

That night in late June, when the group stepped into the light, and found the forgotten world above, life began with a simple campsite. The trouble was they all looked to her for direction.

While inside, they had been mere cattle to the prison warden, Bom. They had struggled against all odds to survive, and with her help, not only had escaped, but now...the eighteen remaining, must carry on. They felt ill-equipped and reluctant to face a world unfamiliar.

Adding to the heavy rejection and mourning she was experiencing, this burden became hers.

She had already resolved, never again would she be remembered as Althea, her birth name from the past; nor would she let them call her Tusha, the favored nickname Loki had placed upon her.

That is a slave term! The past will remain buried; only the present counts, and as for the future, it had yet to be seen.

So, she assumed the nondescript name of Susan.

Their youngest member was of constant annoyance to those exhausted and unfamiliar with children. One day, with tears flooding her eyes, her tiny arms reaching up to the Noor for comfort, Amara's baby, the first born of the freedom fighters as Loki had proclaimed her, said her very first word...Sus. From there, the moniker went to Susa.

Each time the child needed reassurance, she pleaded using that word, and her consoler accepted the innocent moniker.

The rest of the company took it up, and so, the Noor female that led them, became known as Susa. All knew never to call her by another designation, and Susa was as close as they could come to the known familiar, Tusha, they had known her by in the past.

In those first days, she had formed a cabin, only a small one, with two large rooms, one for the men; the second for women. Except for Norris and Downy, who knew what she could do, the group as a whole, thought she had just came upon it in the woods. But as work to prepare a future garden plot proceeded, and implements appeared where and when needed, seemingly out of nowhere, suspicions began to form in the minds of others.

It was one day, in the wee hours just before dawn, as she was forming an addition to house baby and mother, that Susa was caught in her benevolent deeds. Just as she was in deepest concentration, the four women came out to bathe in the river, rounding the corner unexpectedly. The first Susa was aware of them was when she heard Downy shout:

"Don't touch her!"

Susa came back gasping. The shock of dropping from mental to normal thought processing gave her system a jolt of excruciating pain. The logs she'd been raising fell in a heap, tumbling from the wall she had begun, rolling away helter-skelter. And the Noor could hide her talents no longer.

Word went around quickly. She gave up then entirely, trying to disguise what she'd been doing, because, after that, every time she covertly began forming anything, she would come back to reality, only to find a crowd of onlookers behind her, marveling at her feats.

She took to growling at them, ordering them back to work in the garden, or to do laundry...anything, but watching her while she was so vulnerable. Finally, her companions became so used to her using her abilities, they no longer questioned them. Whenever they required a tool or appliance they did not have, they simply asked Susa to make it.

Truly, perhaps, they are becoming too dependent upon me.

And so the complex grew, section by section, until there was space to house at least an additional fifty or sixty new adults, along with twenty infants of various ages.

The men took turns guarding the perimeter, hunting and fishing; the women prepared, stored, saw to meals, and the cleaning and washing. The garden was now flourishing, maintained and harvested on a schedule. All did their part; none slacked off. With a large root cellar, and the smoke house, work and food was plentiful.

Even at the very beginning, none of her flock appeared prepared to leave; most had been in captivity long enough to appreciate fellowship over material possessions and freedom...and they all had their unusual past in common, which any outsider would not understand. They felt safety was in staying together, for each still feared being recaptured.

Many times Susa had been to the nearby city. It was easy for her to teleport there, cloak herself both from sight and sound, if necessary.

When first she had gotten the use of a computer and accessed the internet, she had made a search for her family, but all trace of them had vanished, and as there was a warrant out for her arrest, as an accomplice to the supposed kidnapping of her granddaughter, she decided it best she remain seemingly dead. She no longer resembled the woman that had gone before, and there was little chance of recognition in the region where she now resided.

She accessed her meager savings, manipulating the banking system so the transactions were non-existent, and bought animals for the commune. They now owned half a dozen pigs, two dozen chickens, and a milk cow with a new calf.

The group as a whole, had been ready for another batch of escapees for some time, yet Susa, was yet unwilling, unable, to bring herself to re-enter that horrid prison system in the bowels of the earth.

As a last task, with a belt disguised to resemble the prison drain-belts, she had prepared for her own protection. The unit not only stored extra energy, it could also mimic an actual drain-belt. But, unbeknownst to her attacker, the energy instead of escaping into the ether, was not lost, but instead stored inside the instrument itself. Like a small creature playing possum until danger passed, she could appear injured or even dead...supposedly.

Once the mental heavy challenges of setting up had been conquered, Susa was left with idle time. It brought to the fore something she had held at bay by over taxing her mind.

Loki had left her in a parched no-man's land, in a thirsting vulnerable state, with no relief available. That male Noor, choosing freedom over a life on the run with her, had cowardly forced the condition upon her.

When the near madness hit, which seemed at least once a month, she fled to the grotto she had found, way back in the woods. Here she could scream to her heart's content, and nothing but the echoes answered her.

More than her Noor aloneness, and unmet physical and mental needs, her ability to read the feelings and minds around her, did her in.

In her unreasoning torment, she would claw at the trees until her fingers were raw and bloody, mutilate her form with oozing sores, and slash at the skin leaving angry gaping gouges, until...at last, the hunger of mental and physical needs abated, the loneliness became more bearable, and...what had brought her wrath again to the surface, left her mind.

Then bathing in the shadowed waters until the injuries inflicted healed, and she was again normal, she would repair the destruction she'd done to her surroundings.

Last of all, she would sit down and have a good cry, sobbing in deep wrenching misery, grieving...at the loss of Loki.

To the humans in her charge, she was a pillar of strength, the one to lean on; she never let them see how she struggled or suffered. Her pledge had been to care for them...and to rescue as many others as she could.

But, the people around her often wondered, why she never smiled.

And so, she developed the blocker band, which circled her forehead. It shut off the mind voices, could hold her consciousness and abilities for a short period of time. When wearing it, she could access by mental command, controlling on and off function as needed.

Those around her that noticed, thought it a mere ornament she'd taken to wearing as something to remind her of the Noor peoples.

Susa had never been in a capture scenario since leaving the tunnels, and therefore, neither of her personal protection devices had been extensively tested. Both the belt and headband could as easily fail, as work.

She had always been hesitant to test the belt, as to her mind, it seemed too cruel to inflict what would appear to be her death upon her companions.

In theory, Susa was ready to go back inside...physically and technically, but not emotionally. She was unbelievably terrified.

Memory of the prison conditions and what she had endured there crowded her thoughts. Knowing she would be without light for a long period of time, and that her abilities were much more fine tuned now, she realized the incarcerated beings inside would be an unbearable assault to her psyche; aggression, discomfort and pain, defeat, would be on all sides of her. She would not only see, but feel and experience all that the inmates were enduring...and if madness was a problem in the comfort setting of their compound, she would be most vulnerable below in Bom's world.

Susa was doubtful she could safely survive.

She was aware, if she could ignore her great festering sore, she would have the battle half won.

If I could just get past Loki, and put him behind me...

Clearly going back in is the right thing to do...even if I must relive the memories of our time spent together.

In anger, she resolved:

I am no longer helpless! Never again will I be at the mercy of another!

Wounded pride shouted out to take revenge, but reality brought her back. There was another down in the prison who was doing far more harm.

The pleasure of thwarting Bom in his own establishment, to be his bane, to be the thorn in his side...will be immeasurably satisfying.

And think of all the lives I will save...

Chapter 3

In the far reaches of space a small silver shuttle docked with a clunk against the large city-size medical ship.

In the loading dock bay, Liam stood trembling with pent up anticipation.

My physical is finally here! Loki, is home!

****

Uel was quaking in his skin. Loki had not said a word to him all through the transfer from the prison. The Feline knew, the half-Noor had not been pleased with him for what Uel had instigated with More. For the life of him, he couldn't understand why Loki had even brokered his release.

Uel knew their destination was Loki's foster mother Dia's med ship. On one hand it thrilled him; on the other it terrified.

Am I to be punished or am I being taken on to serve as a physician?

Will Loki pay me back, as I deserve, take his revenge, or be the gentle creature he has always been, and forgive?

And so worrying, Uel trembled.

As the outside panel of the ship slid open, Loki finally spoke, his voice a whisper only Uel could hear.

"Say nothing of what transpired in the prison. If you fail at that, more than just we will forfeit their lives."

Uel was not reassured by his words.

****

Loki stepped down the metal open-back stairs, one step at a time. His ankles were still locked in chains, as were his hands, held together in front. It wasn't easy to balance. He was both weak from the drain-belt about his waist, that confined him, and from malnourishment.

When he swayed precariously, Liam cried out in outrage at seeing him. That's when Loki noticed his mental, and steeled both his feelings in resolve, and closed his mind against him.

Liam must not see what went on in the prison.

Uel followed, in like condition, but for him, it was easier. He only wore the chains; he was younger, and in much better physical condition.

"Say nothing," Loki warned again. "I will do the talking."

****

Liam was so angry at the sight of his physical half, he wanted to thrash out at someone, but apparently the shuttle was unmanned, and took off as soon as the two prisoners were expelled.

Loki stood there as if feeling lost, filthy, in fetters, visibly a battered soul, and his mental cringed.

What have they done to him?

Liam stepped forward rapidly.

This ends now!

He would junction with him and ease the burden quickly, break him from the chains; comfort, console and heal.

But Loki backed away when he neared, and the small feline with him hid behind his back, as if he feared Liam's wrath.

"Leave me alone, brother," Loki said softly. "I am not fit to be one with you."

Liam almost burst into tears. Then, as he too saw wisdom in the physical's words, he steeled himself against his own needs.

"Yes," he agreed. "You need medical care...and a bath. You reek of the prison."

****

Uel was told to sit beside the prone Loki on the flat stretcher platform, as they floated from the arrival area, through the halls, all the way to med center. The Noor physical vehemently objected to lying down, but his brother won the argument in the end.

Now, Uel stood back in the shadows, a distance away from the examining cot, as Liam ordered a mechanical to cut away Loki's chains.

The mechanicals were made to resemble a Feline in every way. It moved and acted as if it were any other cat-being. The only difference from those alive, was this machine did not need nourishment or rest, and it gave unquestioning obedience; nor did any ever rebel.

Loki objected, and drew away from the cutting instrument. "No! Do Uel first!"

As his shackles were being removed, another came up, approaching with evident displeasure, and Uel cringed, expecting an objection, to be punished instead of released.

He is obviously the head Physician. This must be Loki's foster, Kimon.

Although both males were of the feline species, the new arrival was about two inches taller than Uel's five foot four. They differed in other ways, as well. Uel was young, only thirty, considered not much more than a mere adolescent compared to Kimon, for the senior was at least ninety.

Even that was young for their species; the normal life span was at the very least fifteen hundred. Kei, their living queen, was at the age of two thousand.

And Kimon was every inch the director; without debate, in command. He was the mate to Dia, the med ship owner. None was above him; he answered to his partner alone. Whereas, Uel was timid, threatened by his new environment, now that he was out of prison.

"Why is he still chained and in a belt?" demanded the irate head physician, when he came upon Loki.

"He arrived so, Poppa," Liam explained. "Bom's way of rubbing it in."

Kimon hissed with disgust. "Well, get these chains off! Now! Mechanical!"

The machine moved to Loki's ankles, then to his hands. Loki was finally able to spread his stooped shoulders. Kimon moved behind him.

Loki was still handicapped by the drain-belt he wore. It circled his waist; was locked there, the probes inside imbedded deep within his flesh. It could not be opened except with a key, which had remained in the hands of Bom.

"Liam, open the belt!" Kimon ordered.

Apparently, they can override the mechanism.

"No!" Loki objected. "He should not touch yet. It would join us."

"Well, we can't have that, can we? Junction is only for private. Those were my rules!"

Both Loki and Liam answered in unison. "Yes, Poppa."

Uel stifled a laugh of delight.

They are almost like one male. So this is how a conjunctive twin entity acts. It will be a pleasure to watch and learn more about them.

Uel was fascinated. The pair towered over those around them, over eight feet in height, yet there was a humble, submissive attitude about them in the presence of their foster father.

Though they were Noor, the boys were still half Feline, yet the fact was hardly evident. Loki always hid his cat-like ears beneath his thatch of auburn curls, and it seemed, Liam had the same habit, though his hair was both straight and black. And, they each somehow, made their tails vanish.

Other than that, their face, body, hands and feet were very humanoid. Only the short fur upon their neck and backs evidenced their Feline heritage; Loki's a ginger color, while Liam's was silver-white with faint black markings.

I wonder what they'd look like joined?

Uel knew Loki's age to be in the mid sixties, but he also was aware, the normal Noor life span was one of perpetuity.

Just then Kimon took note of Uel.

"Take this one to be cleaned," he ordered of the waiting mechanical. He wrinkled his nose. "They both reek! he added, then as an afterthought instructed farther."When he has been fed, take him to Thor to sleep train as a full medical."

"Full?" Uel exclaimed in surprise.

He had only the education of an attendant, and that was faulty at best, having been taught in a prison facility, where much was not as it should be. He had never hoped for such blessing.

"Oh, thank you, sir. I am ever in your debt."

But Kimon's benevolence was not complete. "You will house and serve in my family nest, male. We have taken you under our protection. Go now! Before I change my mind."

Uel scurried after the mechanical, hardly believing his good fortune.

Then he remembered Loki's warning...and what he had been responsible for at the prison.

Is this Loki's doing; he should hate me. Is this his method of revenge?

****

Loki was cloaking his feelings. Liam didn't much like it.

Why is he being so distant?

"Let me in bro. Let me share."

Loki hissed at his mental half. "I am unfit. You should never be inflicted with my mind again."

Kimon shook his head. "He's not himself. Give him time."

The belt slid from around Loki's waist, and Liam saw him cringe, gasp in pain as the probes pulled from his flesh.

"Bastard, Bom!" growled Liam, brought near to tears by the torment of his physical. "Someday, he will pay!"

"Vengeance is pointless," Loki moaned.

"Oh, but the implementing, would be such sweet reward," Kimon agreed, siding with Liam. "Okay, take him to bathe."

"I prefer to be alone the first time. Please, Poppa."

Kimon nodded.

Liam wondered:

Why is he being so stubborn?

****

The doors slid closed behind Loki, and he was finally in the familiar bathing pools of his childhood home. His foster mother, Dia, had built these for her Noor children. Dia hated water, but had discovered early on, that a Noor needed to bathe to heal. After researching Noor histories, she had copied their facilities.

The huge, treated, recycling, water-filled, rectangular basin was twenty feet across, forty feet wide, and ten feet deep. The side platforms were tiled in blue and circled the enclosure, except for at the far end, where a five foot high, ten foot wide waterfall poured from the back wall.

As he entered the water Loki began to scream, not because the liquid did him harm, or made his many open sores burn, but because, alone at last, he needed to give vent to all his stored frustration. He cried out until his lungs were empty, and his throat sore. Then he tore relentlessly at his skin, wishing mentally, he could make it gouged and festering, as Tusha's had been when she sacrificed for him.

At last, sitting on the lip of the pool, he sobbed like a broken being...in regret, at the loss of his only love...the one he had so naively left behind.

Chapter 4

Reva bask in the sun not expecting anything life changing to happen that day. Her life had already been thrown into chaos, changed irreversibly.

What more can happen to me? I've lost everything; there is nothing more to be taken away.

She sat, one last time, just enjoying the view of the valley and the mountains. The hillside upon which she sat was strewn with flowers, a natural garden among the fields of grass.

Reva had taken one last walk, across fields she had helped her husband harvest for so many years. Memories came back of the countless times she'd driven a truck loaded with grain, to augment his work force, when he was short handed; of other times when she brought meals to the field for that man and his crew, sat on the tailgate, after all were sated, and exchanged small talk with him, because he was reluctant to part abruptly, and return to the dusty and itchy task at hand; she had recollections of his haying the alfalfa, and sitting at his side in the baler to keep him company.

These thoughts were pleasant, yet bittersweet. To think of them now, was like saying goodbye all over again, forever. They brought tears, but she quickly brushed them away.

I am done crying! He's been dead for five years. Time to get on with life.

The man she had loved since her girlhood, had been a hard working farmer...until in his seventy-ninth year. When cancer had been discovered in the colon, it was already too late. He believed, it was due to the fact that when he was younger, he had spilled a toxic chemical all over his body, while loading a weed-killing compound in the sprayer. It had finally come back to haunt him, he said.

From the time of diagnoses, to his death, had taken but four months. Despite the removal of the invasive growth, and chemo therapy, after a month, the cancer had returned, spreading rapidly throughout the body. And inevitably, she had lost her soul mate.

Then, not only left with huge bills, amassed because their extended health insurance would not cover his care, but without her partner, Reva plummeted to utter despair. For weeks after she waited for the grim reaper to take her, as well.

Finally adjusting, she had tried to carry on, but by then, she was nearing eighty herself. As they had been childless, and as the few hands they employed were insufficient to care for the cattle, and do the seeding, she needed more help. This meant she must hire strangers, a cost she was unprepared for.

Neighbors were good that first year, generously harvesting the crops for her without charge, but the year following, their own farms took priority.

They can't be faulted.

Again, she must hire to have her own fields seeded and taken off. The expenses exceeded the gain, leaving her with no surplus.

The cattle had been the first to go, sold off for less than they were worth; then the farm equipment was auctioned; the hands were let go. With the savings gone, there had finally been no choice, but to sell the property.

A year ago, at the age of eighty-four, she had tried for a job at a nearby truck stop. She had thought:

At least I can cook.

Reva knew the owner, who agreed to let her work a shift, while she did some errands. The woman left her in the hands of a younger employee. To discourage Reva, the girl gave her the task of making a milkshake.

"Just put in it whatever comes to mind. That's what we do."

Reva had been slow, not knowing the location of ingredients or equipment, and her overseer went out to the front to serve another customer. Annoyed at having to wait so long, their customer left without his milkshake, and as punishment, Reva was put to washing dirty dishes.

There was an industrial dishwasher, but Reva was told, the larger pots must be scoured before being put into it. So, from two to five, Reva stood at the sink scraping at dried incrusted kettles, and scrubbing countertops caked with day old food.

The owner conveniently stayed away, but phoned just before five. Reva could only hear the young employee's side of the conversation.

"...not worth the weight she carries around."

Reva had always felt proud of her trim figure, and the stamina that had held her in good stead.

"Okay...five cents an hour? That's all she's been worth...I'll tell her. She can come back tomorrow for her wages."

That is the last straw!

Reva didn't wait around to hear the rest of the conversation. She removed her apron, walked out the door, and kept going.

Even fifty years ago, when I was in my thirties, they paid more than five cents an hour!

And if this is a joke, it isn't funny!

Five cents an hour for three hour's work! Fifteen cents?

It had been a most humiliating experience. And, Reva had never gone back to collect.

So today, she sat in a field, saying goodbye to the past. She had sold what she and her husband had worked all their lives to build...and had nothing to show for it. After the papers were signed, and the bank got their share, there was barely enough to cover the remaining bills. Now, her belongings were in storage, and Reva was about to catch a train in just over an hour.

Where she would live was still hazy; her future was a blank page.

As Reva sat reminiscing with tears in her eyes, she became aware of a huge black shadow coming up from behind. At first she thought it just cloud, but soon the silhouette resembled a beast. It came silently, predatorily, until it grabbed her from behind.

She had no time to fight.

Chapter 5

Thor's birth name had been Theeinii, but because it was such a mouthful in any tongue, save Feline, in his early years, he'd been given a nickname by a co-worker. His position on the boards was immensely important, a powerful force behind the scenes of the med ship, so that the human had decided to call him Thor. At the Feline's hissing rejection, the man hurriedly explained. 'The epitaph is meant as a compliment. The original Thor, in human legend, was a mighty thunder god with great power.'

It had appeased and appealed to the huge male, so that he accepted the name, ever after.

Now, he had just past his one hundredth year, and though his long black fur was streaked with grey, he was neither frail, nor lacking in energy. His large frame was as powerful as it had ever been, with a mind as sharp, as when he'd been a young kit.

He'd always had an aptitude for things of a technical bent. Dia had not yet been born when Thor was orphaned at the age of eight. They were just building the med ship that would be her legacy, when the young male was accepted into her clan as extended family. When he was brought to the med ship, the first thing that had been ordered was that Thor be trained in the computer board programs.

He'd grown up with Dia at his side, and many thought he would be her preference as mate, but Thor had always known otherwise. She favored Kimon, though it puzzled him why, as Kimon had such a perchance for anger.

The matter had been clinched when Dia and Kimon had fallen into the hands of the Roog. Upon their rescue, it was evident to all, something untoward had happened between them during their captivity. The two were inseparable ever after.

Thor bore no jealousy; Kimon felt no threat from him, and the three remained fast friends to this very day.

****

It was nearing the end of the shift. Thor was ready to relax, eat and take sleep break. It had been a busy, long session. His finger-like paws flew rapidly across the screen, answering the many last minute queries.

"Thor!" thundered Kimon from the doorway behind.

Used to ignoring Kimon's usual bluster, Thor closed off the last of his pressing communication, then turned slowly toward the head physician.

The thought went through his mind:

Still early...?

"Yes?"

"Dia is heading for the home nest. All the immediate family will be busy for a while yet. I want you to accompany her. With the rash of Roog sightings both in the nearer regions of space, and on the loading docks, every female is at risk. While you are at it, you can be of service to her in the kitchen. You are welcome to join us for the meal. We get home cooked tonight, not replicator food..."

Thor grinned. He was amenable to that, as he both enjoyed Dia's cooking, and would always go for a meal made from scratch, when offered.

"What of the boards? Who will replace me?"

"We can shut down completely; man it from the bed nest. There are no pressing matters...are there?"

"None pending..."

"Okay, then. Go! Dia is already at the lift. I don't want her moving through the guardian quarters without an escort."

Thor nodded, quickly rising.

****

In the kitchen, Thor followed Dia about like he was her young kit, obeying deferentially, toting boiling pots to the sink to be drained, carrying others that were full, and fetching obediently missing ingredients.

In the distance, he heard the outer panel to the huge nest slide open. The female's Noor foster children, and their partners, quietly slipped into the large communal sitting room/bed chamber. At first, he had always wondered why they did not converse, after they were set free from the work environment, as was the habit of other staff, but after a time, it had dawned upon him, these were telepaths. They were communicating among themselves; he just couldn't hear them. Once they were in the presence of non-telepathic Feline, they always respectfully spoke aloud.

"We are home, momma," Liam called out.

"Wash up, then," Dia ordered from the kitchen. "The meal is near ready."

"Do we have time for a complete bath?"

Beside Thor, Dia huffed, and Thor chuckled.

"Don't know why they have such a desire for that liquid," Dia exclaimed beneath her breath.

"You know why, momma," Liam chided, as if he'd heard the soft words, rather than merely read the thought. "Loki is down a bit. Needs the healing moisture..."

"I'll live," Loki's quiet voice objected.

But Dia had a soft spot especially for that one; she always had. And it was even more so, now that he'd been away so long in the prison. "I can keep it warm. Go deep bathe. We'll wait."

Thor had seldom seen inside the two large bathing facilities, as he preferred the normal Feline method of cleansing. The one time he had entered the male side, to inform of a change of plans, he had come upon all the Noor males communally cavorting naked in the great swimming pool. It had made him hiss unexpectedly, being unprepared and fearing such an experience himself. For a great warrior guardian, such as he, to express sudden fear, had left him humiliated, but Liam/Loki had gently comforted him with an empathy of mind that left him warm all over.

Thor still avoided intruding on their privacy, but he knew, the needs were different for a Noor. Unlike Dia, he could understand.

****

While Loki had been away, the nest quarters had been expanded. There were now three sound-proof ante rooms instead of only one: two on the upper floor of the home nest, and one below in storage. As well, the usual large communal bed mat had been separated into two: one to allow for the inclusion of the new mates of the younger generation; the other to bring into closer proximity the immediate serving extended family work staff, which included Thor, and now Uel; and the two Bear, and two Slither protectors, though one or the other of these sentry pairs would usually be absent in any given sleep period.

The room was never completely dark, but a muted light emanated from the ceiling, where special fixtures were hidden behind the paneling, to give the Noor children a perpetual energy source.

Loki was still awake, not in discomfort physically, but unsettled enough emotionally, that sleep did not come easily. From across the mat, he absently watched Neil cuddle behind Twila.

The Human Noor slid his hands across the curve of Twila's belly. Half asleep, she responded with a growl of pure need. Grinning with his success, the two vanished. Neil had jumped them to an ante.

Loki groaned. The scene brought to mind the comfort of Tusha's soft body against him, and the fact he'd left her so cruelly behind. A longing filled him, and he crawled away from Liam, who always lay behind him, even though Loki would not allow cuddle.

He inched away from the others, to an empty shadowed corner near the far wall, where he pounded his betraying abdomen into submission, and then, his back to the sleepers, curled in on himself to hide his misery.

****

Liam awoke with a start, feeling suddenly cold. Realizing his physical had moved, he tried to follow, but as he crawled after, he felt the mental and emotional barriers raised against him, and choosing not to force the issue, remained some distance away.

It grieved him. Loki hadn't allowed junction or cuddle since he'd returned from the prison.

I feel lost; incomplete.

Why won't you let me see, Loki? What hurts you so?

I wouldn't judge. You are part of me.

But there was no evidence that he had been heard.

Soon, Liam slipped away again to troubled slumber, where he dreamed he was eating sharp pointed sewing pins from a bowl. Yet the barbs did not damage his inner workings.

Even though he wasn't the physical, he cried tears in his sleep.

****

From across the way, on the second mat, Thor watched it all. The Slither pair was on watch tonight outside the nest door, and he, though dozing at times, was alert as the inner guard. The sudden interaction between Neil and his partner had started him to awareness.

As Kimon, being head physician, was responsible for their physical and mental health, so also, Thor , as the eldest male in the extended family personal, was charged with the safety and well being of those in the nest. It was his duty to spot problems and trouble, dealing covertly behind the scenes.

From his position behind Uel, the ever alert guardian realized there was something amiss between the physical Noor and his mental. He was disconcerted by what he had seen.

He gave a low almost indiscernible growl of disapproval.

Something needs to be done about this!

But Thor was wise enough to know, he could not go to the physical Noor directly.

In order to work this out...I need to understand what went on in that prison!

The only other that could give him the possible insight was Uel. And as with Loki, the male was reluctant to allow anyone close. He seemed even unfamiliar with the cuddle sleep method, that was practiced among most felines, as if somehow he had never been taught natural ways, or had been raised in the prison exclusively. And Uel was decidedly reserved at giving out confidences.

That too needs to change if this male is to be included into the clan, and retain a healthy status.

Thor resolved, on the morrow, he would corner the new comer, and have a firm talk with him.

Chapter 6

To those he passed on the road, the biker that moved by them, appeared overindulgent. His Ducati monster motorbike was the anniversary edition with gold forks, and a red and chrome body. He proudly gave the thumbs up sign, seeming pleased with himself.

When he stopped for fuel, dressed in tight-fitting black leather pants and matching jacket; sterling silver link chain hanging from his neck; a similar bracelet on his right wrist; and a large Invicta silver and black diver's watch on the other, his manner was one of pomposity.

Beneath the spiked red short cropped hair, a lone silver earring graced his left ear, and on every finger were silver rings; one contained a sapphire, another a ruby, and a third an emerald . His feet were shod in heeled black leather cowboy boots.

The muscled chest was hidden by a black tee shirt with a silver and gold shield emblazoned across the front. It proclaimed in large red letters: 'Conquer the World!'

He said his name was Steven, and he seemed an affable sort of guy, as he chatted with the proprietor while paying for his gas.

"Peace, brother!" he said, making a V with two fingers of his right hand, as he turned his back, and moved out the door.

Then he rode away into the sunset, never to be seen again.

They found his beautiful bike, wrecked, in the middle of a gravel road ten miles away, with no sign of its rider.

****

It was already growing dark when Steven left the pavement. He thought the short cut would save him time, and he wanted to make the small town, where he intended to buy a house, before it got too late.

My dream home is the last thing on my bucket list! Then, no more rebel without a purpose!

In his opinion, he'd wasted twenty-five years trying to find the perfect woman who would be satisfied with him as he was. Going from woman to woman, had not only lost him all that he had, more than once, it had degraded his masculine psyche.

After serving a stint in jail, that had brought him to his senses, he realized he was headed toward disaster. Now that he was free, he resolved, he would live life to the fullest.

The heck with the world! And women in general!

Thirty is not too old to start over!

Illuminated by the headlight, up ahead the shadows between the trees seemed to move.

Is that a cow on the road?

When Steven came close enough to see, and recognized what was really in his path, it was already too late to stop. He braked with his right foot, so the motorcycle would stop instantly, but his grip was too tenuous, and his body momentum sent him over the handle bars anyway. As the giant beast rose up to meet him, Steven flew right into the creature's open arms.

The impact knocked the wind from him, and rendered him senseless.

****

Steven opened his eyes. He was buff naked, except for his boxer shorts. Moaning with the pain of many bruised muscles, he rubbed his dislocated shoulder.

Man! Did I fight that thing?

Peering about at his surroundings, he wondered:

Where am I?

In the semi-darkness, he could just make out he was in some kind of holding cell...

Or is it a cattle pen? It sure smells rank in here.

The offensive odors of urine, feces, and vomit rode the air, but they seemed wafting in from some distance place. The straw beneath him appeared fresh.

From the shadows, a voice spoke: "You awake?"

"Yeah. Who are you?"

"Walid," returned the voice. "But they never use our names in here."

Just then the door gate across the front slid back with a squeal, and the most enormous dog, Steven had ever seen, strode in, walking on its back legs.

It's wearing shorts!

The creature growled, long and insistently. It sounded as if it were trying to speak a sentence in some foreign tongue.

When the humans gave no reaction, a voice from back behind the creature barked a command.

"Your translator's off. They don't understand."

The first beast touched its throat, and suddenly the words came clearly in English.

"Get up! Time to work!"

"Not going anywhere," Steven said rebelliously. "'Till you tell me where I am; what the hell you are; and what gives you the right to kidnap me like this? Oh, and I ain't doing anything with my shoulder out of joint like this!"

"It's no use fighting them," Walid's timid voice cut in. "They are bigger, and they'll kill us without a second thought."

"Too bad..."

"I been here awhile. You don't live long, if you defy them. You want to end up in the meat cages?"

"What are those?"

"Didn't you hear?" yelled the small Arab man. "They eat humans!"

"Cut that jabbering," growled the huge dog. "Git out here!" It turned away toward the hall, talking to the beast in the shadows. "Stupid gibberish! Are they trying to talk?"

"Oh, never mind," his companion returned. "They're not intelligent enough to create a decent sentence."

Steven's jaw dropped in shock.

Are they kidding?

"What are these things?" he asked his companion. "They insult us like that, and I suppose they think, they're the smart ones?"

"They aren't very, but you still better not mess with them. You'll end up on a Roog table, like I said."

The dog in the cell wheeled about angrily. "Silence! I'll have no more back talk! Out here!"

Walid submissively led the way, and Steven decided, until he knew the layout of his environment, it was safest to follow.

****

Flanked by the two big dogs, one on either side of them, they moved through half-lit rock corridors, passing dark open spaces, where Steven distinctly heard the rush of waves crashing against rocks. Then on into a large underground cavern, where stood an enormous arched girder positioned over a huge circular platform on the floor.

"Stand back from the transporter pad," ordered the bossy guard.

The second Roog stepped to a nearby waist-high workstation, and did something on a screen.

"Coming through," he warned.

The huge pad in front of them began to fill with furniture, household appliances, foodstuffs, and boxes of other miscellaneous articles, including clothing.

Bossy dog motioned to a near-by wheeled wagon. "Load it! he ordered." Then the two sentries stood back to observe.

Steven took what seemed the least heavy, his shoulder aching, and right arm useless.

After a time, the Roog that had operated the transporter mainframe, nudged the other.

"Thought you always choose strong ones?"

"I do," the boss dog agreed. "Why?"

"The new one you just brought in is crippled."

His companion grunted in disgust. "Guess it got injured when it slammed into me."

"Maybe we should take it to the med docs?"

"Naw. I can fix it. I worked for a while in med bay. I know just what to do."

Steven let go the small table he'd been dragging with one hand to the wagon, and looked about for a place to escape.

"Seems like it got the drift of what we're saying..."

The boss dog barked what sounded like a laugh. "Catch it, and hold it!"

Steven headed for the tunnel leading out of the room, but though he weaved a zigzag course between the two dogs, they soon cornered him. Struggling against the strong armed being, he was brought to the boss dog with little effort.

"Hold it still!"

Steven yelled involuntarily, as Boss dog grabbed him by his injured arm.

"Now let it go!"

The human was suspended in mid air by the hairy arm around his waist. When it let go, Steven suddenly felt himself plunge toward the floor of the cavern. Except that Boss still held him by his right wrist, which stopped his fall abruptly. Jarringly, the shoulder clunked back into its socket.

The brave biker screamed out his agony, then was dropped to the floor with little regard to further injury. Steven sat where he'd landed, tears in his eyes, now with the added discomfort of a bruised tailbone.

"Now! Do your share of the lifting, human!" ordered the boss dog. "Or I'll send you to the meat cages."

By now, Steven had a pretty good idea what that meant, so he crawled away, stood, and hurriedly joined Walid on the transporter pad. All bravado had been shaken out of him.

Chapter 7

When she came to, Feather Cloud could not remember when she'd been mugged, but she assumed that was why she was laying face down on a smelly straw floor.

At least I still have my pants on, so I can't have been raped.

But oh, every muscle in my body aches!

She rolled to her back, ready to fight if her attacker was anywhere nearby. It was so pitch black she could see very little. It appeared, she was alone in some kind of cattle pen.

Feather wracked her brain trying to recall what had gone on prior to her losing consciousness. She remembered vaguely the huge dog as it towered over her; the obscene idea that it had been wearing shorts.

Ludicrous! The very idea! It's amazing how your mind can deceive you when you're in trouble.

Considering her confusion, she decided it would be best to call, or at least text someone, even if she didn't know where she was.

I know they can locate a person though the cell phone signal.

She sat up, becoming aware her hips and buttocks felt like someone had used her as a football.

Man! I'll be bruised like an abused whore by morning. What did happen to me?

Feather pulled at the back pocket of her jeans, dragging the cell out with some effort. When she flipped it open; and the screen lit up, the native woman frowned, trying to remember how to use it.

What's the matter with me? Can't remember how to text. Did someone spike my coffee?

Behind her, the squeal of the metal gate sliding open hardly registered.

You'd think I was drunk, but I never touch the stuff. Why can't I remember? Was I hit over the head, and now have a concussion?

Shaking the phone as if it were responsible, or could give her instructions, Feather was concentrating on the LED screen, not expecting the blow, as a heavy unyielding body hit her square between the shoulder blades, sprawling her on to her face once again.

She landed hard, the small appliance still clutched in her hand. A muted crack mingled with a second squeal, as the gate was closed again. This time she had heard it.

What the hell is going on?

Now she was pinned down. The body sprawled across her back was, at the very least, that of a full grown woman.

Feather rolled. The other woman moaned, as they landed side-by-side.

"Where am I?" the other wanted to know.

"Don't ask me," the native returned testily. "I just woke up myself."

"Were you sleeping?"

Man! And I thought I was confused.

"What a dumb question. You think I'd be sleeping here?"

"Where are we?" she asked again. "I feel like I've been drugged..."

"Well, welcome to reality. I feel like someone beat the crap out of me."

"But why? What would someone want with me? I'm eighty-five years old!"

Oh man! A senile old white...

Then Feather caught herself, remembering her own confusion upon awakening. She hadn't even been able to figure out her phone.

The phone!

Feather went fumbling, searching through the straw.

Where is it?

When she finally found the flat instrument, she peered at it in the darkness for seconds, then at last, flipped it open. The screen lit up, but the glass was cracked from corner to corner across the face. When she pressed a button, nothing came up.

It's useless!

"You have a cell phone?" the white woman asked stupidly.

She was sitting up now, peering over Feather's shoulder.

"I had a cell phone!" Feather declared disgustedly. "But thanks to you, it's not much good. You broke it!"

"Sorry..."

Conscience pricked at Feather for her attitude. Truth be told, it wasn't any more the old lady's fault, than it was her own. Though it was no excuse, she was upset: firstly, that the phone was destroyed, and second, that she was in captivity. Feather had always prided herself on remaining free. Now, it had been taken out of her hands.

She grunted. "Not really your fault. Whoever chucked us in here is the culprit we should blame." She stuck out her hand. "I'm Feather Cloud. What's your name?"

"I'm Reva," the woman answered, shaking the proffered member. "Sorry. I'm not usually this...ah...muddled."

Feather chuckled dryly. "Me neither. Whatever happens, we at least have each other. Did you see who brought you in?"

"Think my head was funny...I thought it was a giant dog..."

Feather just stared at her.

****

Reva was beside herself, not just shook up with the fact she'd been snatched away, nor even from the pain of the many bruises covering her aged person. Mostly, she was upset at what was, and had been, taking place since she and Feather had come together.

For many hours the two had huddled in a back corner, while every few minutes new people were tossed into the cell with them.

At first, Reva thought the native girl had disbelieved her. Fact was, Reva doubted her own senses. That was until the lights came on, and they plainly saw the giant canines walking upright, carrying their loads, tossing them in the cells.

And that wasn't the worst of it. When the cage had become so full there was no room to stand, they had all been forced out, to wait in line in the stone tunnel, to be processed. With Feather just ahead of Reva, it had taken a while for them to round the bend, but finally they could hear what went on ahead.

They were grading the humans, separating them off into groups. Some they called studs, others breeders, or workers, but the one designation that sent shivers of dread up Reva's spine, was when they called them 'meat'.

What are we; like cattle to them?

Reva was now shaking visibly, in a fog of disbelief and denial, unable to fathom the reality of where she was. For most of her life, she had led a sheltered comfortable life, free of violence, and those who perpetrated such. Taking part in the feeding, milking, and butchering, of the cattle in their possession, was the norm.

She had never considered what it would be like to have the roles reversed. It left her numb in both body and mind.

Just ahead, she could see a seated five foot tall blood hound. It would sniff at each human as they came abreast of it, pronouncing the deadly verdict, sentencing each to life or death.

This just doesn't seem real. Maybe, I'm in the throes of a nightmare?

Feather was now before the dreaded judge. It sniffed, and growled.

"Breeder!"

Reva nearly passed out.

Then Feather was shooed off to another tunnel, and Reva stood alone.

Fear made her heart thunder; her legs felt like rubber, unable to hold her up. The world went silent; Reva never heard her own sentence.

All she knew, was she was not being sent to the line which had swallowed up her new and only friend.

Chapter 8

It was custom, before each day, for the males of the medical center to meet and review any problems. At such a time, plans were made about coming endeavors. This day, after Kimon had departed for the floor, Liam, Loki, Shiveron, Nyle, Thor and Uel lounged lazily, reluctant to go to their perspective duties just yet.

Liam finally broke the silence. "I think I will head again to the Forbidden planet...seeing as my physical has no desire to allow me into his confidence..." His eyes scanned the other with an almost menacing intensity.

Loki dropped his eyes, and would not meet the gaze of his mental. Uel seemed to suddenly feel uncomfortable, as well.

What is it with those two?

Thor had been too busy of late to corner Uel, and probe into what had gone on in the prison.

Thor gave a derisive snort. "While you are there, bring back a female for the new little squirt," he ordered, with a touch of sarcasm. "He is distracted by the females, and if he is to remain in your house nest, he needs one of his own. He's too young to exist easily alone."

Uel's head came up in shocked disbelief, but he came back quickly, with a rejoinder of his own. "Maybe, you should bring one for Thor, as well."

Shiveron burst out laughing.

Nyle spoke up. "What is your reasoning for going?"

Liam sighed. "Last fall, when I rescued two kits, I came across a female...I think she may know where your mother is, or at least, of her."

"Truly?" Nyle sat to attention, hopefully. "After all this time? There has been no sign of her on the board streams."

"That's because, I think she may be too net wise. She's disguised her actions."

"My mother?" Nyle laughed is disbelief. "She had only basic ability when last I saw her."

"There in is the key. Since you last were together, a lot has gone on, and change in your life, has it not?"

Nyle nodded.

"So, could not the same be said of her?"

The room went silent, each one thinking of all that had transpired in the last year.

It was Shiveron who broke the reverie. "What are your intentions?"

"To seek out the human, and follow that lead first...and no Shiveron; you will not be needed."

"And when do you purpose to leave?" Thor queried.

"Directly. I'll need a shuttle. I doubt I can bring back females by jump."

"Best we have at the moment is a hundred passenger."

"Sounds good. Perhaps my hunt with reward me more than one suitable."

"You do realize, what I said was in mere jest...about the females," Thor added, a bit uncomfortably. "As for me; I've been alone all my life. Not likely there's a compatible for me at my age..."

"Oh, you never know...It would be good for you, and you are quite right. Uel does need a companion. It is not easy to exist in a family setting as a lone male. I should know. If I come across a suitable for either of you, perhaps I can persuade her..."

Thor grunted.

How did my words so come back on me like this? He should find one for himself, better!

Liam grinned, and Thor realized he'd been reading him.

"I will have the shuttle stocked and prepare," he stated, to distract from any further discussion.

Liam nodded agreement, then rose to go. As he passed Loki, his face mirrored hope that his physical might give him an in.

"You could come along..." he suggested.

Loki shook his head. "I am not recovered enough to enter that hostile environment just yet." He then once more lowered his eyes in avoidance.

Thor shook his head. He was not fooled; he knew it was all smoke screen, an excuse.

What is wrong between those two? They haven't junctioned since Loki was returned from the prison.

****

When Liam got out beyond Jump center, out of sight of any sensors, he went to speed-mind manipulation. Suddenly, he and his ship were in the Earth's atmosphere; just abruptly there, appearing as if out of thin air.

I know I'll have to use the slow method coming back with passengers, but why take the time now? Why not use my abilities when no one can see it? And light speed never ever has hurt a Noor body.

He landed in a small clearing, in the middle of a forested area, on the west coast of what was known as Canada. It was the closest he dared come to where he'd last encountered the human female.

Now to find Lana.

Liam cloaked the ship, hiding it from human sight, by making it appear invisible. Then he opened his mind, searching to sense where the woman might be.

He swiftly found her...in a padded enclosed cell.

Chapter 9

Reva stood before an Asian man. He seemed to be a captive like herself, yet was in command somehow, for when they'd first been ushered into the huge kitchen, the lead dog had called him Darren. The human answered, and had been understood by the beast.

Again they stood in line, Reva finally calming down with the wait, realizing her designation was not 'meat', as she had feared, but 'worker'. Now it was her turn to receive an assignment.

"What kind of experience do you have?" Darren asked.

"I've worked in a kitchen all my life. I can bake bread, cakes; whatever you want. I can also make stew, cook a roast, or cut up vegetables, fruit. I've even butchered...so I can cut the meat into the proper cuts for..."

Her sentence hung in the air, as Reva looked around her.

What are they doing? Did I just see a human ear on that cutting board?

At every counter, chopping some form of meat, were elderly emaciated workers. Others were at blackened stovetops, stirring huge boiling caldrons filled with some sort of gruel, but not anywhere was there a sign of vegetables, or the pasta usually served with it.

Before Reva could voice a question, Darren pointed to one of the far tables.

"You can work over there," he ordered. "You'll be told what to do."

He then abruptly turned his back to her.

****

"What kind of animal is this? It looks almost..."

"Human," her coworker stated candidly. "What did you think? The dogs only eat human."

Reva stared at the mis-happened shape in her hands. She was not a screamer, or right then, she would have voiced her horror.

"A fetus? This is a human fetus?"

"So what?" the man asked. "I hear up above, females have no qualms to cut them from their bodies. Only difference is they don't eat them. Here, it's common practice to stew them in their mother's milk. It's a delicacy to the Roog palate."

Reva drew back from the countertop, suddenly shaking.

"I wanted children!" Reva defended. "We just couldn't have any."

"Be glad of that," he returned bitterly. "Then there's no one up there to miss you."

Then he twisted the knife even further.

"You'll be eating human soon too, when you are hungry enough," he continued mercilessly. "What do you think is in the stew?"

Oh, god! Oh, god!

Reva stood there, swallowing bile, trying desperately not to lose her last meal.

I will never eat any of that! What am I going to do? I can't eat human meat. I'm not a cannibal!

Her stomach roiled; her hand went to her mouth.

"Get back to work!" growled the other. "You don't work; you don't get fed!"

Reva stepped back just in time, as she was sick all over the floor.

****

"That new one is bawling beneath the tables," a male worker told Darren. "She refuses to continue. Won't eat either..."

"I'll deal with her."

As the other returned to his station, the Asian approached the sobbing woman. He stood over her thinking.

The sensitive ones are always like this at first. The only way to meet it, is with harsh measures.

Reva looked up at him, her eyes swimming with tears. "I just can't do this," she moaned.

"Would you rather I put you on the menu for tonight's orgy?"

"What?"

"You were chosen worker. Be glad you were considered undesirable as meat. They hunt them through the tables in their eating hall. When they catch them, they torture them... Sometimes, they even eat them live. That's how the warden, Bom, likes them. He plays with them in his quarters. I hear he has some of them clamped to the walls of a torture chamber. Others are held by a neck chain and shackled to posts in the floor...should I go on?"

Reva shook her head.

"Okay, then. Do you intend to do what's required of you in these kitchens, or should I put you in the meat cages?"

The woman swallowed hard, then slowly stood up.

"I'll work," she said meekly.

"Good choice!" Darren turned toward another section, and pointed. "See that bread machine? I've changed my mind. I think you'll do better working back there."

Her face brightened visibly.

"Go now! Before I change my mind."

****

It seemed, Feather had been fighting them forever. And now, they were winning.

She had refused to eat their horrid gruel. Fruit was provided, but it was mostly oranges and bananas.

Too much sugar and starch all at once. Not good to eat too many at a time.

Now, she was paying the price.

In a fog-like state, as if from a distance, she heard the voice of the guards, as they entered the cell. She'd missed the squeal of the opening gate.

"This one should be ready for breeding shortly," said one.

"It doesn't appear normal," objected the other. "It's sweating; breathing too rapidly."

"It's fear. Panic. I've seen it before," declared the other. "She'll be heat overtaken in just a bit."

"That's if she ingested the drugs..."

"We injected some into the fruit, just to make sure."

The second one laughed. Then Feather was lifted bodily and carried.

****

Head pounding, ears buzzing; eyes out of focus; her heart was tripping like a tap dancer.

So thirsty. Tired. Can't get my air...

"Fere...an...I?"

Her speech sounded slurred even to her own ears.

"Now, honey. Don't you worry none. I'm the one does all the work..."

She was naked. Her fingers were numb; so were her feet, but still she felt his body lower over her, tense, and begin jerking spasmodically.

Feather slipped away, to float in some distant existence, far from reality.

****

As Bom strode through the med bay, Zaba yelled at him. The Root, a tree-like being, was his head physician in the prison establishment, charged with the care of the cattle.

As the creature approached, Bom saw he had a human suspended by her hair, from his long fingered branch-like hand.

"What do you want me to do with this one?"

Bom watched the limp female swinging in mid air. It wasn't even resisting, seemed in some sort of trance-like state. He knew the Root would not bring a piece of meat to his attention without good reason.

"Explain!" he demanded.

"It's a cow from breeding. Been fighting the whole time, but when it came time for impregnation, it did not respond to the drugs; went into coma instead. It's no good for breeding, and not healthy enough to put with the workers, or into the food chain..."

"What's wrong with it?"

"Diseased. What humans class as a diabetic."

"Not good to eat, then?"

Zaba shrugged. "May be good to play with...it fights like a she bitch when conscious."

Bom grinned, and stepped closer to examine the listless thing. The female was slim, well muscled. She seemed of native heritage, with the long dark hair and brown skin tone. It was young, maybe, about late twenties.

Too bad. She would have made a good breeder.

He was struck suddenly with an idea, as the Root had hoped he would be.

"Can you fix it enough to make it a challenge again?"

"I can cure the disease with a fetal tissue implant," Zaba agreed. "It'll be like new."

"Don't care how it's done," growled Bom, anticipation rising in his breast. "Give it what it needs to be healthy. I am in need of a female toy to play with. Chain it in my playroom when you are finished."

Zaba grunted. "As good as done! Give me ten hours."

"No problem. I'm hungry, anyway. Time to find me some meat!"

Bom turned on his heel.

As he moved through the swinging double doors, he was not plagued in the slightest by qualms of conscience. The fact that he had just sentenced an intelligent being to spend the remainder of its life as his hunted prey, didn't even faze him.

Chapter 10

"Bom's hunting again," Nuff warned Boss dog as they let the human cargo haulers out of their pens. "You'd better bring them back early this night, or lose them again."

Boss dog growled low in his throat. "I wish that cat would stop stalking my workers. I just get them trained, and he has to eat them on me. Why can't he feast on the ones from the meat cages like everyone else?"

"Likes to catch them himself. They say he plays with his food. Must be from his Feline side..."

As Steven took off after Walid, he was thinking about what he had just heard.

The first time he had seen Bom, he had realized why the other Roog called him cat. Not only was he a monster, towering above the others at eight feet tall, but he appeared to be a mixture of both dog and cat. His face and head was that of a bulldog, but the body, with its shaggy black coat, and matted bushy tail, was that of a Feline. His feet had no extended claws; they were hidden, and even on his front paws, the weapons could be retracted. It was rumored, Bom could gut a full grown enemy with one swift slice downward.

Steven had learned quite quickly what kind of place he was in. He'd taken supplies past the meat cages, and he never wanted to land in one.

He'd also seen where they kept the studs, and even if those guys did have better food, Steven wanted nothing to do with forcefully breeding any woman.

For jeepers sake! I thought we were civilized men! Not dumb cattle!

He had seen the lives of the others here, how the women were treated...especially the pregnant girls...

Here they have it horrible...beyond cruel! Downright barbaric!

But that's how it was done in this godforsaken place.

He vowed, never again would he take advantage of the opposite sex.

He'd also delivered stores to the kitchens, the storage rooms, and the med center. It had given him an education he would never forget.

After seeing what went into the gruel, Steven would only eat the bread and drink water. Occasionally, he stole fruit from packets they delivered.

As far as I'm concerned, loading cargo is just fine...for now. Until I can find the way out...

He and Walid went about mostly unsupervised now; they had the run of the place, but as far as Steven could tell, there was no way out.

****

"Run!" yelled Walid. "Hide!"

"Why?" Steven wanted to know.

"I just saw Bom at the end of the corridor!"

Steven backed up behind the flat of clothing they were hauling, but Walid took off back down the tunnel. Suddenly, Bom was descending toward Steven. He ducked through a nearby doorway, as the giant beast sped past him.

He expected, he'd never see Walid again.

****

Steven had spent the night in the vacant food store, curled up in a large tub of soft garments. It was the best sleep he'd had since he'd been captured.

He heard More, the old Root creature that ran the establishment, lumber in. There wasn't time to hide, as the tree-like being came past him.

More stopped short; moaned like a disembodied spirit. "No! No!" he shouted. "Get out! Shoo! No humans in here. More not need trouble, you hear? Go! Go!"

And Steven clambered out, as quickly as he was able. At the door, he peered around the corner. The tunnel appeared empty, so he made a dash for it.

He sped past the flat of clothing, that had remained where he and Walid had left it; down the long silent tunnel, just as it went bright, as the morning lights came on.

Steven was hungry. He wondered if Boss dog was feeding the others, as he usually did.

Will they let me back in to load, and deliver the cargo, as before?

Did Bom catch up to Walid? Is he dead?

If he is, will Nuff give me another partner, or send me to the meat cages?

Suddenly, life seemed uncertain again; it didn't feel quite so promising.

Around the bend Steven ran, heading for the cages of the freight workers, hoping against hope he was still worker, and not the supper meal. As he passed a still darkened side tunnel, he failed to see the narrow tree branch beneath his feet.

By rights, down this low in the earth, it shouldn't have even been there, but it was. The paw that held it, was quick and malicious.

Steven tripped, falling face first into the dry dust of the corridor.

For an instant only, did he sense the towering dog above him. Just as Steven turned his head to see, a giant foot pressed down hard upon his left ear, pinning him to the earth.

The huge fist seemed to come out of nowhere, slamming the top of his head. Next thing the biker knew, he was being dragged by a leg, like a sack of limp produce, down the side tunnel he'd ignored.

The ride was bumpy, and Steven's head whammed violently against the granite wall more than once. The second time it happened, all sound and feeling fled; lights appeared inside his head, then vanished, to be replaced by oblivion.

Chapter 11

These white walls, the starched bed linens; they are too clean!

Lana lay on the white cot bored beyond belief. At least, back in the breeder cells, she'd had company, and someone to talk to, but here alone in this bright, clean, padded room, there was nothing but her memories.

The psychiatrist believed her whole story was a fabrication, a figment of her imagination, made up because she felt guilty at being pregnant without the father to provide for her.

But he's wrong! So out to lunch! If he went through half what I did, he'd mess himself.

She almost missed the dirty cattle pens, down in the bowels of the earth, she'd been there that long. They had taken her as a girl of thirteen.

It's Tusha's fault I'm in here now! It all started going wrong when she showed up!

By the time the old lady, Althea, had arrived in breeding, Lana had forgotten more about the upper world than she remembered: mother, father, relatives, friends; these were shadows of another life. Existence consisted of bearing, and to be carrying, meant better food. When you were large enough, you were even allowed comfort. That had been something to strive for.

Lana had fought for supremacy, taken from those weaker, always the aggressor. Even with the senior...she had won out.

Or so she had thought!

Lana hadn't realized who Tusha was, when first she saw her again, but the night she came to rescue her friend, Beth, when recognition had dawned, Lana realized, she was the aged breeder, Althea, whom she had thought she had gotten rid of. The woman had been trouble from the start!

What happened? How did that old hag come back as a new young thing? And how did she come by those crazy powers she possessed?

But even her hidden talents couldn't save the kid. I got even with the enemy in the end; in the tunnel above, on the way out! Yes, I did!

How bad the woman had been hurting over the death of the teenager. Even Loki was unable to fix the wounding grief.

Lana cackled to herself.

I won! Yes in the end, I'll always win!

But the trap had sprung again.

Never mind! It doesn't matter. The Roog have me tagged, from that night in the park, but no one is the wiser. Sure, Bom always knows where I am now, but he has no further use for me.

Even though that man Liam had taken her to the clinic, and they'd kept her in the hospital until her eyes were healed, the doctors had never found the implant.

They never will!

But, no matter what she did, Lana seemed destined to forever be in captivity.

She remembered well, the morning of the day after she'd gotten released from hospital. The night before had been raining, so she spent it in an abandoned car, curled up with a musty blanket she found on the back seat. The battered wreck, in the car graveyard beside the highway, had been one of many.

What made the cops search the very section I was in?

****

The crack of a Billy club against the side window jarred her to shocked wakefulness. Her first thought was, she'd been found by the vicious dog creatures from below, again.

Lana gazed about in confusion, uncertain of where she was.

What is this place?

Through the glass, someone was yelling.

"Miss? We need you to open up. You can't stay in here! Will you roll down the window, so we can at least talk?"

It was then she noticed the uniformed woman standing outside her tiny sanctuary. Lana couldn't remember how to open the door.

"Roll down the window, please?" the woman shouted.

"I...I don't know how?"

"See the pull button at the bottom of the window?" The officer pointed, and as Lana followed her gaze, reaching for the button, the other woman instructed: "Yes. That's it. Now, pull it up."

Lana obeyed without thinking. Almost as quickly, as she released the popup, the door was rapidly yanked open, and Lana roughly pulled to her feet. The movement made the world spin, and she passed out, before she could say a word.

****

"She's coming too," a voice said from a distance.

"She's pregnant. If I'd realized that, I'd have been more gentle."

"Expectant women can be dangerous too. Don't beat yourself up."

There were two of them. Earlier, Lana had failed to see the guy standing back behind the woman. Now, he was down on one knee, before her, concern written on his features, but eyes still wary. This time it was the woman cop standing back at a distance.

Lana sat up slowly. She'd been laying on the back seat of the police cruiser, the door open.

"What's your name?" the male officer asked.

"Lana." She ran her tongue over dry cracked lips.

"Okay, Lana. When was the last time you had something to eat?"

"Yesterday morning..."

"Well, we'll have to remedy that. Where do you live?"

"I live here...in the upper world."

Lana knew that was the wrong answer, as soon as it escaped her lips.

The man stood up, frowning, looking down at her as if she had plague.

"What do you mean by that? Where are you from?"

He towered over her, authoritative and menacing, worrying the Billy stick attached to his belt. Lana sank back, fearful.

"I come from under..."

In the hospital she had managed to deflect questions like this. They had never asked directly: where she lived; what her name was? They had called her Jane Doe, thinking she had not just lost her sight, but also her memory.

Even the social worker, assigned to her case, had assumed her to have been misused by a boyfriend. And when a mix up in paper work had resulted in her being discharge, Lana had been quick to escape the premises.

But now, she was in hot water again.

Time to fabricate a story.

But unfamiliar with this above world, Lana floundered again.

"I just got out of hospital..."

"What kind of hospital?" The man wasn't about to give her an inch.

"There is more than one?"

"I think we'd better bring her in while we investigate," suggested the female officer.

"Think you're right," he agreed, closing the door.

****

Lana heard the click of the deadbolt on the only door into her padded room. She sat up.

Meal time! Good!

"You going to give me trouble, Lana?" asked the orderly, as he stepped in with the loaded tray.

Lana shook her head. Many times she'd fought them, hoping to escape, but that had only gotten her drugged up, and in a straight jacket. She preferred to have some semblance of freedom.

"You know what you get, you try anything?"

Lana nodded.

"Okay then." He set the tray on her night stand, picked up a small pill cup, and the glass of water, handing the pills to her. "In they go."

Lana had tried before, but she had to make another attempt. The pills went into her mouth, under her tongue. He handed her the water glass, and she took a sip, pretending to swallow the medication.

"Open up!" Lana opened her mouth wide, keeping the tongue down. "Lift the tongue." Groaning, she complied. "Lana!" he warned.

She swallowed the pills.

Setting the water glass down, he turned to leave. "Make sure you eat everything," he warned, as he went out the door.

****

At first the jail cell wasn't half bad. It reminded her of the breeding kennels. She was fed; she had a place to sleep...they even supplied her with her own place to eliminate.

What more could I ask for?

But when they moved her into a hospital again, Lana didn't much like it. This time, she wasn't allowed to wander around. So she threw a temper tantrum.

She tossed the chair across the room; they put her into restraints. When they let her loose again, she waited docilely until the second night. While everyone thought her sleeping, she quietly went to the closet, took down a coat hanger, and behind the closed door of the bathroom, rammed it up inside her.

The next morning they found her, biting into the flesh of her miscarried fetus.

And since then, she'd been in this padded cell.

****

The male nurse had just left her room with the empty lunch tray. Lana sat up, rose from the bed, and began to pace.

I'm getting absolutely stir crazy with no one to talk to.

She'd been given craft supplies, but never a knife or a scissors, for fear she would take her own life.

What's a person suppose to do with paper, pencils, brushes, and paint? They said, to put my thoughts down; draw what I'm thinking. If I painted pictures of where I've been, now wouldn't that freak them out?

She wheeled toward the barred window, and drew back startled. Before her stood the most handsome creature she'd seen in a long time, part cat and part humanoid.

"Who are you? How'd you get in here?"

Then it dawned on her.

Except for the black hair, he looks just like Loki!

"Ready to leave this place, Lana?" he asked.

The voice was that of the man, Liam, and Lana laughed delighted.

"Never so ready in my life!"

"Will you think of where your journey in the upper world began?"

Her mind went immediately to that dark night over a year ago, to the exit hole, as she had stepped into the fresh air.

He took her by the hand, and jumped them. But instead of the rocky field at the edge of the forest, where they expected to go, they reappeared on a teleport pad in the bowels of the planet.

And the ferocious demon dogs were all around them.

Chapter 12

Steven didn't want to open his eyes. His head was pounding like a kettle drum being played in a rapid percussion. He moaned, long, drawn out, and plaintively.

He tried to open one eye; it was half swollen shut. The other wouldn't open at all.

Where am I now?

It seemed he was strapped to a wall by his wrists and ankles, spread eagle, in the form of an X. And he was buff naked.

Man! This isn't the worker kennel.

He looked about him. The light was bright and made him squint, but dimly he saw to his feet. A young native woman lay just a few feet away, chained by a neck collar and long rusty chain, to a post in the floor. Her hands were tied in front of her, and she too wore nothing but her birthday suit. She seemed unhurt, but appeared to be napping.

Rather than draw attention to himself by shouting, which might bring their jailer, Steven tried to see across the room. What met his eyes, sent shivers of horror through his aching body.

It appeared to be a pile of meat on the dirt floor in the corner, but was actually the remains of a half eaten man. The arms and legs were missing; the head was still intact. Though it was absent the garments, Steven recognized who it was.

Walid! My god...Walid. Oh, man; oh, man! I'm in deep shit. This is Bom's feeding place. Man! It's over for me, for sure.

Bom strode in, and the girl awoke with a start, whimpered, and then went silent, as the beast walked past her, to stand directly before Steven.

"No meat gets away from me!" the mixed breed creature growled. "I hunt until I capture; Then I eat my fill. You are fortunate I am sated."

Steven wasn't so sure it was beneficial.

"But, I have need of entertainment before I retire. Which human should I play with? The male or the female?"

Steven cowed against the wall, but there was nowhere to go. He saw the girl beyond them, cringe in dread, hold her breath, as if awaiting the first blow.

Bom raised his paw-like hand toward Steven's face. The claws were extended. But just before the sharp talons struck, the room filled with the most ominous sounds, not bells exactly, but a clanging and shriek that froze the blood of any that heard it.

At first the beast's face showed annoyance, then sudden comprehension. In one swift movement, he dropped his arm, and spun on his heel. Bom was gone from the room in seconds.

Both Steven and the girl expelled the breath they had been holding. They had a reprieve, but was it any better to hold them in trepidation, awaiting the next encounter?

****

Bom strode rapidly to his private teleport pad, anger and anticipation warring within him. There was only one reason the warning would sound.

That Noor has come back for his she!

And Bom had prepared for this. He had known all along the rebellious cow was the key. She had disappeared along with the butterfly.

So, he'd prepared the bait.

He had sent his soldiers above to find both females, but they had come across only the one.

At least they got the tag on her, even if they did lose sight of the cow, afterward.

The tag was a complicated instrument, yet operated quite simply. He knew where the human was at all times.

The small red dot on his board told of its whereabouts, but he'd left her thinking she was free. At some point, he reasoned, either the butterfly one would make contact, or the Noor male would show up.

Bom had been patient.

And it just paid off!

Bom had placed around-the-clock rotating sentries near the teleport pad. The tag was programmed to redirect any effort to jump the subject.

The Roog half breed moved through the doorway with determination, his weapon wand in hand. First thing he saw, was the battle raging before him.

Bom had deliberately shielded the chamber so the Noor couldn't teleport out again. He was trapped once they had him within the prison walls.

The human female lay stunned to the side. The Noor was fighting a manual battle, conserving his energy, not using his powers, with the hope of escaping with his last bit of light reserve.

Like a pack of primitive wolves, the snapping, snarling Roog warriors had the larger being surrounded. The Noor had shape-shifted to a cat-like form and was clawing, hissing and spitting defensively. He might have done much damage had the dogs let him close, but they stayed just out of his reach, unless they could get behind him, and take advantage of his unprotected behind quarter. The fight seemed at a stalemate.

Bom raised the wand. It was set, prepared to deal with a fully powered Noor. He fired. The Noor male dropped like a rock with the first ray.

"Put him back in a drain belt, then strip him, and strap him to the wall in my quarters," he ordered curtly. "I'll deal with this wayward cow, myself."

****

Light years away, Loki was crossing the med bay floor with a tray of sterilized instruments for Kimon. He was mere feet away from the head physician when it happened.

Loki stopped abruptly in his tracks. "Bom has him," he muttered, half under his breath.

Kimon spun. "What was that?"

He watched as if viewing in slow motion. The giant Noor healer folded, as if all the energy had been drained from his body. Instruments and tray hit the floor with a cacophony of sound, and scattered about the fallen male.

Suddenly, the Feline surgeon was yelling in panic, angry and frightened by what he could not explain, calling for mechanicals to come to his aid.

Is he ill? I've never seen him go down this sudden before..not unless a weapon has been used.

I knew Liam should not have left. Loki hasn't been right, since he came back from the prison.

The two mechanical robots appeared at his side, and Kimon ordered tersely: "Put him on a power bed. His energy must be raised without delay."

Minutes after the bed had been powered up, Loki's eyes fluttered open. He gazed about, confused and disoriented.

"What happened?"

"I was hoping you could tell me," returned his foster father. "You went down like someone used a drain wand on you."

Loki looked away, refusing to meet Kimon's concerned gaze.

Kimon hissed, annoyed. Whenever his children avoided eye contact, he knew they were hiding something.

"Do you want to tell me what is going on?" he demanded. "Or must I punish?"

The threat was only superficial under the circumstances, but it was his only recourse.

The giant male remained silent.

Why must they keep secrets? Do they not trust me, after all this time?

"Look at me, Loki!" thundered Kimon, angrily. "If something is wrong, I need to know!"

Loki finally met his gaze. "Nothing you can do, anyway, Poppa..."

"Let me be the judge of that!" the physician fired back. "Now, tell me what you sense."

"Liam..."

"Liam what?"

"I think...he's fallen into Bom's hands."

Kimon hissed in a breath of dread, then steeled himself with resolve. "We'll send a ship after him!"

"Be too late, Poppa."

Kimon groaned. He knew his Noor fosters were uncannily accurate when they assessed a situation.

"The best we can hope for is that Liam might outwit Bom, and get free on his own."

Kimon nodded, hope rising at the words. "And what of you?"

"As long as Liam and I are separate, Bom cannot kill us. I may suffer consequences, but as long as I still breathe, Liam lives."

"Okay, then!" Kimon decided. "You rest."

"I need to keep busy," Loki said, attempting to rise.

Kimon pushed him back. "Remain on the bed until your energy is up."

Loki settled back, and closed his eyes.

He must be feeling pretty bad not to argue the point.

****

"Thor!" Kimon demanded. "I need a private word with you."

The board technician rose and followed the other male. Once they were in the nearest ante, Kimon broached the problem on his mind.

"Liam has been captured by Bom. I want you to take a warp drive shuttle to the Forbidden planet; find his ship. If it is still intact, and hidden, I want you to wait and be available when my son frees himself. He may not be in the best condition."

"You don't want me to go inside the prison?"

"I need no more of my staff as Bom's playthings."

Thor nodded. "What of the boards? With Liam gone, and me also..."

"Shiveron and Nyle have become proficient enough they can handle it together."

As Thor turned to go, Kimon added: "Take the new one, Uel, with you. He might be of use, as he is familiar with the Roog and their ways."

"Yes sir." After a moment, Thor voiced what he'd been thinking. "You do realize, it could take me weeks before I get there? Liam could be dead by then. am I to keep a channel open for communication?"

Kimon shook his head. "Unwise. Roog will pick up the signals. That will put you in danger. Silence is best. Return only when you know what has become of the young one."

"If I can..."

"His ship was equipped with the sensor to detect a Noor gleam, was it not?" Thor nodded. "Find him!"

Chapter 13

As Liam slowly became aware, he first felt the light. He guessed rightly, it was so bright, to ensure he might be revived.

He had never, ever, experienced this exhausted, queasy, physical loss of energy in his life. Loki had always been the one to take on any corporal punishment that was meted out to them. His physical had endured all the bodily pain, each of them believing, he was better suited to handle it. Suddenly, Liam regretted the fact he'd allowed that without assisting, withdrawing when the encounter took place.

I've been an egotistical, pompous, insensitive, uninformed mental, thinking I knew the answer to everything, because I was the greater mind. What possessed me to think, because Loki is only physical, that he was unwise, and nothing could damage him...that hurt was easy for him to bear? No more! From now on, Loki, I promise, I will take my share, undergo life's hardest knocks with, and for you!

Liam groaned aloud. An effort driven from deep inside.

At his waist, even before he opened his eyes, Liam felt the penetrating probes of the drain belt piercing his innards, draining away any chance to store energy. Only the bare necessity of life-giving light was allowed through.

And it hurt, excruciatingly so, numbing his senses in body, soul, and mind.

And Loki endured this for nearly a year?

Liam wanted to kill that Dog/Feline, Bom!

He drew in a careful, painful breath, and finally, opened his eyes. He expected his nemesis, but, though he was not alone in the room, Liam saw nothing of the prison warden.

Fastened to an iron frame, against a steel wall, at neck, wrists, and ankles, Liam was obviously helpless. A human man was fastened across from him, the male's eyes half closed, swollen shut by some blow, the face black and blue against the tanned yet pale caste of his skin. His body also was covered in scrapes and bruises. Viewing the human's nakedness, Liam realized he, himself, had been stripped, as well...and, he had no mental capability to manipulate replacement garments, due to the energy drain.

At their feet, was a darker skinned human female, her long dark hair shielding some of her own nude private areas. She seemed unharmed in body, but was trembling with unrestrained fear. Wide awake, she watched him, and for a second, he read in her mind, curiosity, and wonderment, the idea and hope, that perhaps, he might be a savior.

Liam knew, he couldn't even save himself, just now.

His gaze panned beyond them. Appalled, he noticed the half eaten human in the corner. A shiver ran through him.

Then suddenly, Bom was in his face, standing as tall as he, big as life, before him.

"Welcome to my playroom, Noor." Bom declared, venom dripping from his words. "In all your time in this prison facility, I never got to bring you here. Nice of you to come back to rescue this little human she, so I can have a talk with you in private."

He thinks I am Loki? Has he never seen us together?

"Do you want me to demonstrate my methods on these hapless cattle first, or would you like a round, right off?"

Liam chose not to answer, preferring to let the Roog-half keep his misconceptions, until he realized, he wasn't dealing with a slow physical's mind.

Liam turned his eyes again to their feet. It was then he noticed, there were two human females, both chained by a neck collar and chain to posts in the floor, each equally bound, hands before them. Lana was the second, and her naked body was already covered in bruises, as she knelt at their feet.

Why does he leave their legs unbound?

He had no further time to wonder.

"So you think silence will work, eh? Oh, I remember your lack of response from before, Noor. It got you nowhere last time! Remember, what it got you? I nearly killed you that time!"

This time Bom had his attention! Liam raised his eyes, and probed the dog's mind, and what he saw there, brought his body to shaking anger.

But, Bom mistook his trembling for fear.

"Yes!" he exclaimed excitedly. "I know! I can kill you! If it hadn't been for your butterfly, I'd have accomplished it before. I owe your little vixen, payback. Where did you hide her?"

Liam rebelled at the thought of searching that revolting mind again for the answers he needed, so he simply disregarded the attempted provocation.

"Okay then! I guess you need a demonstration. How about I use this one, brought in with you? You seem so fond of the little cow."

Liam reacted with shock and horror, as he read the intent of the Roog cat.

"No!" he objected vehemently. "Your fight is with me!"

"Oh, but then, I would have no fun. I'll do you both. Wait your turn now...I need to stimulant the juices with pleasure. I haven't slept, so must replace my lack with hunger..."

****

Lana fought back with all the hatred and anger stored inside her. She clawed, even with her bound hands, at the mighty hairy arm of her attacker, bit down hard, deep, when she connected with the flesh of the beast.

Bom yelped at the affliction, growled, and batted her hard across the face, till she let go, then laughed, as she sprawled flat on the dirt floor.

"That's it; fight me!" Bom thundered exuberantly. "Give me the enjoyment of the conquest. Fight, little she! Fight me, with all your might!"

And Lana obliged, with every ounce of her strength. He pulled her hair; she swore with the pain. Bom bit down on a leg; Lana kicked him in the teeth.

In the background, she could hear Liam screaming at her attacker.

"Leave her be, Bom!" he cried, his voice holding regret. It was as if he was blaming himself for their imprisonment.

But, this crazy warden and I go way back!

"Your fight is with me!"

"Yes! It is, Noor!" Bom agreed. "And, I will indeed finish with you, but not before I have pulverized this rebellious one, and taught her, she must never cross this dog!"

The fight went on and on. Occasionally, the Roog giant turned the wounding weapon in his hand on the male strapped against the wall, just to include the rescuer, and make certain he too paid an adequate price for his interference. The beam tore through the flesh of the male to the very bone, each time it was used.

But the interlude, gave the girl on the floor a breather, so she might gain strength to fight again. Then Bom was back, fighting like a cat worrying at a toy, shaking her, tossing her, just as violently, as he had before.

She fought, until the energy, finally, suddenly, went out of her, like a light bulb blinking out.

Lana slumped to the floor, torn, bleeding, spent. Bom stepped back.

She made one last effort to crawl away. Bom watched her, as if he meant to let her escape. Seconds passed. Then suddenly, he stepped forward, stomped down hard upon the curve of her back.

There was a resounding crack, that made those watching cringe. Lana felt her extremities go numb. And mercifully, the scene before her eyes fled away.

****

"And now, it's your turn!" Bom growled, turning toward the Noor...

Chapter 14

Reva had just been told to go on a lunch break. Her favorite spot to get away to do this, was in the empty corner, behind the large bread making machine. Here, there was a large six foot square empty section, that just seemed meant to hide away in.

She had never questioned how come it was there, or why others avoided it.

She picked an apple, made herself a sandwich with bread, wilted lettuce, and tomatoes, then filled her bottle with water. Reva made for the corner sanctuary.

As she rounded the corner, she drew up short in shocked surprise. It was already occupied. It had never been before.

In the remote corner, back in the shadows, sat a woman of about sixty plus, younger than most others that staffed the kitchens. She had her eyes closed, as if sleeping. Reva had the distinct feeling the woman was recovering from some recent trauma, though she had not the foggiest idea why she felt that way.

On either side of this new human, were two enormous, heavy-looking backpacks. These appeared to be empty.

What impressed Reva the most, was the incredible beauty of the woman. She was neither thin nor obese, so she was not from the kitchen or an escapee from the meat cages. Appearing quite healthy, and robust, as if she was used to strenuous work, she was well muscled, and curvaceous, with a figure the envy of any younger woman.

Her silver white short cropped hair curled about her ears, with wayward locks seemingly windblown and unkempt. Around her forehead, she wore a circular head band, which only peeked out in sections, almost invisible, because it was of silver.

Another factor that made Reva doubt the lady had been down here long, was both she and her clothing were fairly clean.

The eyes of the stranger opened slowly, and Reva felt mesmerized by the depth of blue in them, as they calmly took note of her.

"I didn't realize anyone used this place to sleep?" Reva rebuked, daringly.

The woman nodded, as if she already was familiar with the ways of the kitchens. "Tell Darren, I am here. Now! Please."

Reva frowned at the authority in her voice. "Are you...not suppose to be in here?"

"I am not a prisoner... Go. Please, do as I've asked."

Reva placed her lunch on the dirt floor. "Don't you eat my meal while I'm gone."

The woman grunted disparagingly. "You must be fairly new?"

Reva sighed. "Been here about two weeks..."

"You'll not survive, if you trust another prisoner...especially where food is concerned."

Reva eyed her suspiciously.

What would she know about it, if she's not from down here?

"I will not take your sandwich," the other reassured. "Please. Get Darren for me."

Reva decided to trust her word. Besides, Darren should know what was going on, anyway. She turned, and went to seek the Asian overseer.

****

Darren turned, when Reva tugged at his sleeve.

"What?" he demanded, in annoyance.

Reva pulled him close, so she could whisper in his ear.

"There is a woman back behind the bread machine; says she wants you."

Darren frowned. "Why?"

Reva shrugged. "She's giving orders, like she's somebody important."

Darren thought a moment.

Is someone sick? Or do we have an escapee?

Suddenly, an unexpected thought occurred to him.

Couldn't be! Not after all this time.

"What's she look like?"

"Clean. She's a beauty; wears a headband of silver."

Darren's heart leap to his throat. He turned, and ran rapidly toward the corner where the bread maker stood, Reva following at a quick walk behind him.

****

Reva didn't want to miss this.

Bet he bawls her out but good, for being here.

But when they slipped behind the huge machine, into the empty space, Darren dropped to his knees in awe.

"Tusha... We all thought you must be dead."

"Don't call me that," admonish the new comer. "I prefer not to be reminded... I have changed my name... It is now Susan."

He chuckled. "Ha! You couldn't find one that sounds more exotic?"

A fleeting half smile fled across her features. "Nice to see you, too."

"Ah, Tus...Sus... Goodness, what do I call you?"

"Guess, Susa will do. That's what Amara's baby calls me." She patted the ground beside her, encouraging him to sit. "Easier for me," she explained. "I won't have to look up so far."

He laughed, and moved over beside her. "We...I missed you. Aw, it seems so long since I've seen a friendly face. Must be almost a year now. I'd near given up someone would come..."

"Had to set things up...took a bit."

He nodded, quietly admiring her.

"Do you think I could have some fruit...and water," she pleaded. "I used up what I had on the way in. And maybe you could restock the backpacks with food...please?"

"Reva!"

The old woman jumped, at the sudden curt command.

"Get an orange, and..."

"Bottles are in the packs..." Susa supplied.

"Well, don't just stand there! Jump to it, woman!" Darren growled impatiently. "We have a very important guest. Hop to it!"

Reva turned slowly to obey.

"Don't forget the bottle for the water." Darren motioned to the nearest backpack. "And when you've brought the food and water, start replenishing the packs she came with."

"With what, sir?"

"Fruit, bread, sandwiches..."

"Meat?"

Susa growled low in her throat, like a caged animal, at mention of the word.

"No, no human meat! And, don't forget, lots of water. She'll need lots of water. Fill one of the large water vessels they use to carry to the hospital." He added, turning to the visitor: "One of the meat guys can carry it for you."

Reva dropped to the nearest rucksack, opened it, slipped out the bottle, and fled.

"I'm taking out as many as possible," she heard the woman say behind her. "We can handle at least fifty, twice that, if we double up. We may not get to come again..."

What are they planning? She talks as if she came in from up above. How did she get in? And what does she mean, take what? Who? Is there a way out of here?

****

When Reva returned with the second restocked backpack, Susa was quietly finishing her orange, while

Darren soberly watched her in silence. He seemed to be brooding over something.

After placing her burden beside the new arrival, Reva stepped back, stood waiting unnoticed.

Susa looked up at her, but seemed to address Darren instead.

"I'll take those left in the meat cages..."

Darren nodded, quietly.

"You sure you don't want to come?"

Darren shook his head. "I can follow later. Which way is the right way? Left or right?"

"Right."

"Someone has to stay behind," he reasoned. "All hell will break out down here when they discover... I can best deflect and buy you time. I did it the last time..."

"There may not be another chance, Darren. Bom may take it out on you..."

"Can't think of a more honorable cause."

His confidant shook her head, half disagreeing, but she allowed the statement to pass.

"Begin sending them up as soon as they arrive." He nodded. "Can I have one of your kitchen staff? I need a companion...to help with the pregnant ones...in case one gives birth on the way."

"How about this one? I can do without her; she's too delicate to work in here..."

"Not the stomach for it?"

"Right!"

"What's your name, dear?"

"Reva."

"Okay. Reva, you will wait for me, here. Don't go without me...until I..."

Darren broke in, obviously concerned about something, not realizing he'd cut her off in mid sentence. "Susa? Bom has..."

The woman frowned.

"In his playroom, Bom has..."

"Spit it out!" she ordered impatiently.

"He has...Lana. They recaptured her...yesterday."

Susa drew in her breath, as if she was viewing something horrific from his mind.

"I think, she's near death, by now. I've heard the dogs talking, betting how much longer they'll live. Loki..."

Susa growled disapproval again at the name.

"Sorry..."

"Don't mention him!"

"Well...anyway, I think Bom's recaptured him, as well."

Susa hissed. Then sat thinking. Finally, she broke the silence.

"I'll check it out."

She rose to her feet, and simply vanished. Even Darren seemed surprised at her sudden disappearance.

Chapter 15

Loki sank to his knees with exhaustion and pain. His skin was covered with welts and bruises. He knew Liam was fairing far worse, but there was nothing he could do to help...except give of his extraordinary energy-strength, from a distance.

It seemed, Kimon just appeared before him, but the Noor knew his foster had no such abilities. Loki's awareness was simply dulled, to the point of inattentiveness.

"Go to the home nest, Loki," Kimon ordered compassionately, a rare occurrence for him. Then he shouted angrily: "Uel! Uel! Come and help Loki!"

When the slight Feline slunk forward, expecting to be berated, the head physician even softened his brusque manner for him. "Help Loki to our nest. See that he bathes, even if you have to get in the water with him."

Loki knew, Uel liked the water, but the male would never let on to the headmaster. He'd been without it so long in the prison, he actually found it pleasant. Gladly, he supported Loki, and they shuffled to the elevators.

To Loki, as they arrived, it seemed they were dream walking. The pool was so far away, and he felt so absolutely wiped. Uel guided him to the edge, let his legs dangle, while he actually did get in the liquid to pull off the leggings.

He hissed in consternation. "Why are you so full of festering sores? What's happening here, Loki?"

Like a lost abandoned child, Loki burst into tears. "I should have stayed with her," he blubbered. "I should have warned him... It would have been better had I died by Bom's hand... than keep this awful secret."

"Oh, Noor...friend. You did what you thought best for the moment. I don't know what went on...and you don't seem to want to tell me, but...it must have been real bad for you to get like this."

Loki suddenly realized he wasn't making sense. Uel deserved some explanation.

"I...I'm like this...because...cause, Bom...now, has Liam. We are a conjunctive entity. He and I are one being..."

"Eh?"

The way Uel screwed up his face, caused Loki to burst out laughing, which only made the Feline all the more certain, this Noor was missing some of his faculties.

Loki steadied himself. Laughter was good; heightened the spirits.

"I...we, are a twin creature..."

"Eh?" Uel said again. "And just what is that? Never heard of it."

"It's a Noor condition. A male is born who can separate into two parts, a mental and a physical, but both look equally like a single being."

"I been trained medic, but was never taught that."

"That's because you didn't need it. It's Noor medicine. And Liam/Loki is the only one of his kind."

"Okay. They say Noor cannot be untruthful. If your brain is not addled..."

Loki grinned. "Not lying. Not that addled."

"Okay. So why you suffering?"

"I am the physical...the feeling part...the strength..."

"So...let me get this straight? You are feeling what's happening to Liam?"

"Bright Feline! You'll make a good physician, someday."

"Don't humor me, male. We been together through too much to treat each other badly."

Loki sighed. "True."

"Besides, I owe you. I'd probably be dead now, if you hadn't spoken for me." The dripping wet Feline crawled out on the ledge to sit beside the other. "So, what's Bom doing to Liam? Torturing him?"

"Yes."

"And...nothing can be done?"

Loki shook his head. "Liam is probably in much worse shape than I..."

"Bummer! I've half a mind to go back there, and take that half-dog to task."

"Well, you'd better change that attitude if you're coming with me!" Neither male had heard the doors slide open and shut again. Thor stood just inside the entry. "Kimon said, I'd find you here. You are to come with me, Uel. And you'd better be willing to obey orders without question."

"Where we going?" Uel asked apprehensively.

"We been ordered to wait for Liam to free himself."

"The Forbidden planet!" squealed Uel fearfully. As long as there was no chance he'd ever go back, it was easy to be brave. "Bom will kill me!"

"Not if you stay out of his way. Now come, I need your help. You know the planet."

"But I don't! Besides, Kimon told me to take care of Loki."

"The Noor will be better when he bathes. He does it quite well on his own. You! Come! I'll brook no argument!"

Whining plaintively, Uel followed the elder, and Loki was left alone with his thoughts.

****

Susa stood in the hallway leading to the first breeder stalls. By force of will she released the door locks on every gate. There were hundreds of women, but she knew not all of them would take the bid for freedom. They had been reduced to a cattle-like mentality.

They simply do not understand what is at stake, and I cannot force them all to take advantage of my offer.

Projecting the mental command, she ordered:

"If you desire your freedom, go to the kitchens. They will tell you what to do. If you want life for the child within you, go immediately. Be very quiet, or you will bring the guards down upon you. Spread the word as you go."

Their lives are in their own hands now. I've given them the choice; done all I can for now.

She'd given the same offer to those left in the meat stalls.

With a sigh, Susa turned toward Bom's quarters. She did not relish facing Loki again. In her opinion, far too much time had passed, and too many things had happened since, for their love to be rekindled, but it wasn't in her to abandon anyone. The fact remained, she still owed him her life.

****

Standing invisible outside Bom's lodgings, Susa reached out with her mind to sense that obnoxious presence. He was in the corner of the darkened far room, curled upon his side, on a sleep mat of straw. His sleep was the deep, exhausted stupor of the spent, but she knew, he could come alert with the slightest sound. That was the way of dogs; one minute snoring, the next awake, vicious and snarling.

But, Bom is also cat. He can be sneaky, quiet and stalking, when he pounces.

I'll need to be real careful.

But neither was it wise to place a shield to silence her actions. It took too much energy, and Susa had little enough in this down-under dark place.

She fingered the belt beneath her clothing, upping the power button to draw in a higher level of energy from the bulbs above. Lights all down the corridor dimmed, blinked out, then slowly flickered back.

The room within was brightly lit.

He's prepared that torture chamber for a Noor, but never-the-less, it's beneficial to me. My belt will store quickly, power up to full capacity. That might mean the difference to my survival.

Valiantly, she stepped across the threshold.

Her first sight was of the Noor male strapped against the wall, battered, bleeding, seemingly unconscious. Her heart flipped in empathy, but deliberately, she turned her back, so she would not be tempted to go to him.

Susa took in the others imprisoned with him; a human man hung against the opposite wall, merely badly bruised and naked. Apparently, Bom hadn't gotten to him yet.

She'd forgotten how ugly nude human men looked.

At least Feline and Noor males have their manhood hidden away inside.

Shivering with revulsion, she turned her back to that creature, as well.

On the floor at her feet were three posts imbedded in the floor, each with a chain attached, at the end of which was a neck collar. One was empty, the other two each held a human woman captive.

The first, a beautiful young native, with long dark hair, had tears on her cheeks, and was trembling visibly, but seemed unharmed. The second, she barely recognized. It had to be Lana.

None present, were aware of her entrance into the room.

Susa moved to her nemesis, appalled at her condition.

I wouldn't wish this, even on my worst enemy!

Susa fazed to visibility.

Chapter 16

He was dreaming of icy cold winds against his face, and snow pleasantly falling. He'd seen snow only once, on a rescue, where he'd brought home three tiny kits, orphaned by the Roog.

Liam sensed the power of a Noor gleam nearby.

Surely, Loki wouldn't be so foolish as to attempt a rescue? He knows, if Bom gets us together we are lost.

Bloody drool dripped from the corner of his lips, and he sucked in a agonizing breath before closing his mouth. Some of his ribs were broken, causing excruciating pain with each intake.

He opened swollen eyelids, which remained half closed due to the angry blows from Bom's brutal fists. Liam knew, his face must look like that of the black and blue human across from him.

The room was the same; the three humans: one on the wall, another at his feet, and...the dying one. Except, now...Bom had finally gone to the inner chamber to sleep, and at last, left him alone. That half-Roog had spent himself with his violent endeavors to destroy the Noor he hated so much.

Liam looked about searchingly, wondering. Still, he felt the powerful presence of another Noor. But, the prisoners seemed alone in the room.

Must have been dreaming...

And the realization dashed hope; his mood plummeting drastically.

Then before his dimmed vision, an image began to form, the first memory of which his fevered brain would remember as long as he lived.

Standing beside Lana, a humanoid-like female slowly materialized. Approximately, five foot three, she had a figure of exceptional curvaceous beauty, which she had attempted to hide with loose fitting garments.

Liam could only see the back of her wavy silver-haired head, and a partial side view, but she took the breath from him, and filled him with such a carnal need, he had to dampen the desperate desire by sheer arduous willpower.

He immediately realized, his reaction was inappropriate to the occasion, but his body was determined to betray him. He did his best to turn his thoughts to other matters, but even then, it took a moment before he was again in control.

If the female was aware of him, she gave no inkling.

Must be my drained physical condition that has me so susceptible. I've never been attracted to a female in my life. I am...a mental! Only my compatible should elicit such need.

He watched as the Noor female knelt, gathering the battered Lana to her bosom...

****

Susa folded the broken human into her arms, moaning over what had been done to her. Lana looked like someone had repeatedly smashed her with a huge meat tenderizer mallet; every bone that could be broken seemed to have suffered trauma; no part of her skin was without cut or bruise; eyes were swollen and black; the nose was broken; teeth missing, and lips bloody. The woman drew breath with exceeding effort.

I wouldn't wish this on my worst enemy!

And yes, dear Lana, you once were my adversary. But, no more! We need peace... forgiveness between us...no more battles!

Lana tried to open her eyes, as if sensing Susa's desire to heal. Lids half swollen shut, whites bloodshot, the mirrors pleaded for mercy.

"Oh, don't...try...to mend me," groaned the dying woman. "Leave me be...old woman. You... you...can't save me... Just, let me go. Let me...die in peace...Tusha. No...more...vengeance! Just... let me go! No...more..."

Tears filled the eyes of the other, spilled down the smooth flawless cheeks.

"Lana..." Susa groaned.

"Forgive...me," whispered the battered one. "That's...all...I...ask."

"Oh, Lana. I never was your enemy. Be at peace. I forgive you. Circumstances made you what you were...and what you did, proved beneficial in the end."

"I...sor...ry," Lana gasped.

Her frame stiffened with a last effort to stay, to say more, then slowly the life faded from the eyes, and they became blank mirrors; the body went limp.

Was she just waiting to die in my arms?

Quietly, Susa began to sob; the room went distant as in her grief the Noor woman remembered their first meeting, the trials endured together. And she cried, brokenly, for what might have been, cradling a would-be, lost friend.

Vaguely, she thought she heard someone yell a warning. Bom seemed to come out of nowhere. Then his wicked weapon drained every ounce of power and energy from her.

****

Liam moaned at the sight. He'd yelled to warn, but she had not reacted on time.

Why did she ever come in here? It was a trap! No sane creature would have been this selfless. What a waste!

Bom was ripping the garments from the unconscious form, slicing the sleeves with his open claws, tearing away the soft leggings, leaving her exposed for all to see. The Roog-half laughed, delighted.

"I wondered," muttered Bom. "She's wearing a drain belt. Stupid butterfly! Always knew this one wasn't all there." He turned to Liam, gloating. "Did she try the belt in memory of you, and then couldn't get out of it?" He chuckled. "Well Noor, now you can watch her die...but I'm much too tired to do it now."

Laughing still, Bom freed the dead human carcass, tossed it away in the corner with the half eaten male, then proceeded to chain the one he called butterfly.

"You can watch her for me while I sleep, Noor." Bom chortled again. "I'll see you all, after sleep break."

Then he sauntered confidently from the room.

Liam looked down on the fair form. He now saw why the Roog/Feline called her butterfly. On the outside of her left hand was tattooed a tiny blue butterfly.

She was the most beautiful being he had ever seen. Just visible on her back was a sheen of soft white fur from waist to just below her fine white-silver curls, and folded, near hidden, just behind her shoulder blades were...

Are those tiny wings developing?

His eyes roved unbidden down the length of her torso. Laying on her side, the lower knee bent, the upper leg spread out straight to the side, she looked so vulnerable. It was then, he noticed, the birthmark on her open right thigh, a small heart-shaped rose-colored, barely visible blemish.

A healer mark! Loki is the only other one who has one like that. But, his is on the left. That means she is an Instant Healer! I never knew there was another. Female Instant Healers are said to be extremely powerful.

If this is fact, the loss of her would be doubly tragic.

****

Hours had passed. Liam was near giving up hope there would ever be movement in the female. All at once, her image shimmered. Suddenly, she was fully clothed again.

Liam drew in a sharp breath of anticipation, and wonder.

How did she accomplish that?

The chain at her neck dropped away; the bounds about her wrists vanished. The small Noor being got to her feet, walked deliberately over to stand directly before him, and stood looking up, regarding him with piercing blue eyes. A second later, the pupils turned to vertical ecliptic cat's eyes. The center expanded, and went to ever changing hues of rainbow colors.

Liam felt mesmerized, hypnotized. Before he could stop her, she had slipped into his mind.

He felt her rapidly gathering and copying all knowledge he held. With a gasp, he tried uselessly to fend off the intrusion, but to no avail. And though she raked his brain for its content, he could not reciprocate, gleaning nothing in return from the mind behind the assault. He could not even enter hers; it was blocked from him.

He had never encountered a mind more powerful than his own!

****

Susa knew instantly the moment she entered his thoughts.

This is not Loki?

At first sight of him, she had assumed his physical appearance had changed some since they'd parted. Noting now, the difference in the hair coloring, she went deeper, to familiarize with the man himself.

Liam! Okay? Loki said, he was only a half. This must be the other, the missing piece. And... he knows nothing of what went on in the prison, or of me. Loki has kept silent.

Mentally, she hissed with frustration, cloaking her own mind, so he wouldn't learn such answers from her.

Why, Loki? What did you fear in telling your mental what happened?

It didn't take long to find the answer, see the rules broken. Even if this male knew nothing of what had transpired, he was a treasure trove of information.

Chapter 17

After Susa had gleaned all she could from his mind, instead of speaking to Liam, she turned away, and walked to the trembling, naked human chained at their feet. Dropping to her knees before the other woman, she reached out reassuringly, to touch not only her physical form, but also her psyche.

"I am, Susa," she revealed, speaking in perfect Na-Dene. "You are called, Feather Cloud?"

Tears formed in the girl's eyes. "Oh, help me, please..." the woman begged plaintively.

"Do not fear me, please," Susa encouraged. "I will set you free. Don't be alarmed by what happens; I don't intend to hurt you."

"Bom, will hear," Feather whispered in English.

Susa switched to that tongue, knowing the dog/Feline did not understand it well. To him the words in any human language was like the mewling of a cat to the ears of mankind.

"I am aware of him. He sleeps soundly, and understands little of human words. They are a background noise to his ears, but...it is wise to be quiet.

"Lie still for a minute."

Susa willed the changes.

Immediately, the neck collar fell away; the bounds on the woman's hands vanished; and a light shift covered her nakedness. Her long black hair was suddenly in a braid at her back.

"Oh, thank you," breathed the woman in gratitude.

She sat up, but swayed dizzily.

"Take it slow," cautioned Susa. "We need to go, but give me a moment, to see if the coast is clear."

The Noor woman stepped stealthily to the doorway, standing quietly, listening. All was silent. She reached out by mind, to view Bom one last time. He slept the slumber of one content with his world.

"Okay." Susa motioned for the aboriginal woman to follow.

"I can't feel my legs. I can't stand," Feather said in panic.

Susa turned back into the room. Moving quickly to the other's side, she helped her to her feet. "As you walk, feeling will come back."

When they moved toward the outer hall, Feather moaned. "They feel like they're filled with pins and needles."

"It will pass quickly.

****

"And, will you leave me to fend for myself, female?" Liam asked evenly, from the wall.

Susa paused.

"Perhaps, males so foolish as to come unprepared, who fall into traps...deserve what befalls them?" she returned, without turning about.

"I was searching for you..."

Gently, the woman lowered the younger girl to a seated position against the wall beside the doorway.

"I know that," Susa declared, turning to face him. "Who says, I wanted to be found?"

"I know there are too many males in the universe, and you could have your pick of any, but are you so heartless, you would leave one to die?"

She stepped nearer him, studied him boldly, knowing full well he was propositioning her. Her coyness surprised him, caught him off guard, and again a desperate need filled him. It was as if this female was the only one in the universe, and he desperately wanted to be hers.

What is wrong with me? Have I become a physical?

Her eyes mirrored amusement, and he realized, she knew the effect she was having on him, though still, he could not see into her mind.

I always can read others. Why can't I read her? Am I that energy depleted?

"Perhaps," she said, after a moment. "You could serve some purpose." She turned her head, looking toward Feather, yet still talking to him. "Are you willing to help this woman? She has been without food too long."

"I'll be glad to carry her..." He decided to play hard to get, to bargain. "If you will set me free..."

"Will you also obey me...without questions?"

"As any male of my species would provide for a female, I will serve you diligently."

Susa gave a short mirthless laugh, as if the thought was an absurdity; stood studying him, still. Suddenly, she turned serious.

"I doubt you'll be able to carry a full grown woman..."

The neck band holding him split apart silently. One wrist at a time opened, and immediately he forcefully rubbed the numb appendages together to increase circulation. Next came the ankles. When he stepped down, he fell to his knees unsteadily. She reached out to support him.

She certainly has more strength than I do at the moment. I feel like a toddling infant trying to gain my feet.

How embarrassing, for one who should be a gallant warrior!

"Help each other." Susa motioned toward the woman near the doorway. "Head for the kitchens. The Roog will be waking soon."

****

She stood in the empty doorway, watching after the two that had gone, as if she was sensing where the enemy lurked. Steven felt abandoned, utterly hopeless.

She means to leave me behind. Do I have to beg like he did?

"Please...don't leave me behind," he pleaded, from the wall where he was fettered, helpless. "Please...have some mercy. Don't leave me here alone with Bom."

The woman turned, moved back into the room, stepped over to him, and hissed venomously. "I have no fondness for studs! They prey upon helpless women without the least compunction or compassion, enjoying their cruel bestiality, no matter the consequences to others, so no! I do not rescue them! Bom, can have you!"

Tears of horror and fear sprang to his eyes. His heart thundered in his chest.

She's my last chance! Why is it my fate is always in the hands of a woman?

Anger tore to the surface. "I'm not a stud! I was a worker; loading cargo off the transporter..."

She laughed derisively in his face. "You say, you are no stud? What were you before you came here?"

That brought him up short.

She let the words hang in the air a moment, then went on. "How many women, Steven?"

How can she know? What is she?

"I am a telepath," she answered. "You can have no secrets from me!"

The silence in the room felt oppressive. Steven had been rendered speechless.

"Do you think a relationship with a woman is only one sided? Think you, she is just there for your pleasure, and has no intelligence beyond her need? You are no better than the studs in here!"

Steven's temper surfaced once again , as he fired back. "Every last one of the women used me!" he yelled. "They took everything from me, judged me wanting, and tossed me away."

"Now, I wonder why?" she returned quietly, sarcasm dripping from every word. "Did you ever give them respect? Were you sympathetic when they cried? How often was your every word a put down? In your eyes, you were always the better person; the smarter mind. Did you ever give them even a chance to show what they could do?"

"I loved them..." he declared lamely.

"Right!" She turned from him. "And every self-absorbed, self-indulgent individual deserves the wakeup call you are now experiencing."

Steven groaned. He knew, it was all true. Thinking fast, he came back with the only answer possible. "You're right! I know I was an A hole, but I've learned my lesson. I'll do better. Please ...don't be so heartless. Don't leave me here!"

But the woman simply kept on walking.

He tried one last-ditch effort. "You're no better than the rest of the aliens in here!" he yelled maliciously.

The first inkling she had softened, came in the form of a pair of shorts that suddenly appeared over his exposed privates. Steven would have laughed, if he hadn't been so petrified.

So the lady doesn't like to see a man naked?. Well, tough! What kind of B is she anyway?

Then he remembered, she could read his mind, and he cringed, feeling suddenly defeated.

Abruptly, the bands about his wrists and ankles snapped open. Steven dropped like a dead weight. His legs were numbed of feeling, and so he fell forward to his knees.

From the door, just as she went around the corner, Susa ordered: "I'll be watching you, Steven. Keep up, or take the consequences."

The first few yards, he crawled. Then, as feeling brought the pins and needles to his lower extremities, Steven made it shakily to his feet. With sheer effort of will, he made his limbs move under him, and ran with all his might toward the kitchens.

Chapter 18

When Susa entered, the large room seemed mostly empty. Only a handful of humans remained, at the cutting boards and stirring the huge cauldrons on the stoves. Darren and Reva stood to one side, with Liam and Feather.

Panting, Steven joined her. Susa stepped across to the others, paying no mind to the taller human at her side.

"How many?" she asked Darren.

"You have only one hundred ten..."

"No more?"

Darren shook his head. "Seventy pregnant; some meat, and those who wanted to go from in here."

"Have they all gone up?"

"Yes, all but these new ones, the Noor male, and...you. The packs and water still need to go, as well. Wasn't sure what you wanted done with those."

"I'll carry the packs," offered Liam.

"One," Susa agreed. "I'll carry the other." He didn't argue. "And this useless human beside me is used to carrying heavy loads. Give him the water tank."

"Steven?" question Darren in surprise.

"I believe that is his name."

"He has always been quite beneficial..."

Susa ignored Darren's attempt at praise.

"You sure, you won't come with us, Darren?"

"What good would I be up there?" Darren blustered visibly. "Been down here half my adult life." Then he softened his tone. "I've covered you before; I can do it again."

"We may not get to come back..."

"Go!" Darren became firm, commanding. "Go on! Get going! Don't worry about me. I'll see you next time, and if not..."

Susa stepped forward, and hugged the small Asian man. They parted; his cheeks blushing a dark shade of crimson.

"Okay. Up with you, Reva. Take Feather, and show her the way. Then you, Liam..."

"No," the Noor male objected. "I follow you. It is custom: Female first; guardian behind."

She wasn't about to enforce her will. This wasn't the time for it.

"Up, Steven. Follow the women, and you'll need good balance with that tank upon your back."

Simply to goad him, she deliberately pretended unconcern for his welfare. "We wouldn't want to lose the water."

Steven grunted his displeasure, as he put his arms in the straps, to shoulder the heavy container.

****

Reva had watched the others climb the wall. From below, it had looked so easy. You couldn't see the handholds, nor where they led. But now, as she rose up, each indentation was at just the right position for hand and foot. The only difficulty, was not to look down.

She was not normally afraid of heights, but the granite walls were greasy, and she fleetingly wondered why no one else had plunged to their deaths.

Perhaps, it is because they each so desperately want freedom.

At first Reva had waited patiently, but after hours had passed, she had near started up after the others, without permission. Even Darren had seemed worried, appearing to think something unanticipated had happened to Susa.

Then the big cat-like man had stumbled into the room, supported by and yet, also helping her friend, Feather, whom she thought she'd never see again. The man was so obviously injured, mutilated by ugly, ragged open lacerations, extensive bruising, with black and blue shiners about both eyes; it was hard to deny, he'd been the one Bom had tortured.

The man was breathing with great difficulty, the sunken side of his chest evidence of more than one broken or cracked rib. Yet, he made no sound of complaint, only stepped back away from Darren, preventing any sudden painful contact, as the Asian approached to greet him.

At first Darren had called the being, Loki, but the other had simply explained, he was the mental half, Liam.

That really had made no sense to Reva, at the time.

It appeared, the second arrival, Feather, was merely exhausted, weak from lack of food. She was physically unharmed, which was rare in this underground hell. Darren saw to it, she was given bread, and some water to sustain her.

Liam refused the same, when it was offered to him. The man simply stood quietly waiting, anxiously watching for Susa.

Then the creature all awaited, the one responsible for their rescue, burst through the tunnel entrance with a human man in tow.

And now, at last, Reva was ascending toward freedom.

At the top of the hidden escape route up the wall, she found a large hole. The eighty five year old woman was not a heavy person, and she fit through easily, climbing into smoky darkness. Feather followed. Then came Steven, balancing the soft plastic barrel-bag of water strapped to his back.

Finally, Liam's head rose above the opening, just after Susa had climbed in.

"Move along the tunnel," Susa ordered impatiently. "Quickly! It is less smoky around the bend."

Reva and Feather hurried to obey.

****

Bom was furious. He'd awakened to empty breeder pens, and worst of all...his personal playthings had all escaped.

Should have know. Never trust a Noor! They always have some hidden means to thwart me!

"Open the stud cages!" he ordered angrily. "Maybe, some of those males know the route to the passage that seems so to elude us. If not, at the very least, we will have an enjoyable hunt and delicious feed."

"But then we'll be left with no stock," objected his prison supervisor. "We'll have to start all over..."

"Time for new stock, anyway," declared Bom. "About time we hunted more aggressively on the surface. Humans above are too complacent. Time to show them we exist!"

****

From the doorway of his produce store, More watched the goings on with some trepidation. The tunnels, usually empty this early in the day, were crawling with activity. Naked human males were everywhere, while their handlers quietly hunted, yet did not pounce.

What goes on here? Has the end of things finally come?

May be time for More to cut his losses, and go above to the Noor Queen?

But maybe, wait and watch first...see who wins. Then More travel to Loki!

****

Darren had such a heavy premonition of impending doom, he could hardly breathe.

Whatever possessed me to remain behind? Need my head examined! You think you are invincible, Darren?

He shuddered, as the din in the tunnels grew closer by the minute.

Suddenly, the kitchens were inundated with naked men. As the humans weaved through the cutting tables searching an escape, some stopped uncertainly, realizing they were not only trapped, but no longer privileged and above the rest, immune from attack. Now each was the same as those hunted for their meat. Terrified, panic stricken, others sought for the path of departure, milling about in circles, where the dogs cornered them, waiting.

Do they expect these pampered men to know where the exit is?

I am the only one who knows that!

I must keep these brutes down here! The secret will die with me!

And so Darren joined the panicked crowd, with an astonishing bravery he'd never known was in him, ripping away at his clothes, tearing off the translator from around his throat, so that he would be just another among the horde.

At least my death will be quick, if not merciful!

Those preparing the food were cast aside, some falling, to be trampled underfoot, others scattering, hiding, while the Roog chased the hapless, helpless ones, and fear and panic ruled. Strident screams filled the air, vicious snarls from the hunters, the gurgle of death escaping throats, as the cattle were ferociously conquered.

Then Bom, angrily hunting the headman, came upon Darren. To him all unclothed humans appeared the same, and he failed to recognize the one he sought. If he had, he would have spared him now, and strapped him to his torture wall, played with the useless animal, until it spilled the knowledge stored in its little brain.

But, this shrunken chested, scrawny piece of flesh in front of him, enraged Bom, though he knew not why.

The Roog/Feline caught the creature up in one deadly paw, and with the other eviscerated the defenseless human, just because he was in his way.

Chapter 19

He had never known such darkness. Liam had to clench his teeth until they ached, just to keep the sudden madness at bay, that the lack of light energy was bringing on. If he had not known that Susa had come in this way, and been half Feline himself, he would have pushed aside the slow moving human line ahead of them, and fled to the surface more rapidly.

There were now one hundred and fifteen souls in this upper, narrow and confined, escape tunnel, each one shuffling forward hesitantly at a snail's pace: the meat men and women, overly obese, and reeking still, from being in cages used not only to house them, but as latrines for those billeted above them. These were starved individuals, not use to moving excessively, easily exhausted, and at Susa's suggestion, interspaced, and each charged with helping a pregnant woman, who in some cases, was hardly able to stand on her own either. A slow procession at best.

The heat of these tunnels was also a factor. It did not so much bother the Noor pair, as their body temperature was much higher than that of the humans, but many walking before them would stop to rest often, delaying and impeding the move forward.

It was these many rest stops, that nearly drove Liam over the brink. It seemed there was no end, or way out ahead. Walking behind Susa, ever silent and watchful to their rear, in case they were followed, he wondered why the lack of light did not seem to bother her. Danger was ever present, from behind and before, and the longer it took to get out, the harder to bear. He felt ill prepared to meet any attack should it come.

The awareness of the carnage below came with jarring clarity to both of them.

****

Even travelling in the impenetrable darkness of the tunnel, Susa knew the instant it happened. She went rigid with the shock of it. In her empathetic communion, she felt the very throws of the Asian's life as it ebbed away, and pulled in a sharp breath of disbelief, and agony, at the violent end of her onetime friend.

At that same instant, the Noor male beside her shivered, apparently unfamiliar with the brutal slaughter of humankind, and though he was in a drain belt, and in exceeding pain himself, he too had sensed the deaths beneath them. The male however, being only a mental, did not feel as deeply as the Instant Healer female.

As Bom finished his despicable deed by snapping the neck, and Darren's life essence escaped this world, Susa sank weakly to her knees, dropped her face into her hands, and burst into hot tears.

Suddenly, Liam was kneeling beside her. Despite his grievous wounds, the utter agony of touch to him, he reached around her, and enfolded her against him.

For long seconds, she enjoyed the comfort he gave, the pleasurable feel of one of her own kind intimately sharing, then she pulled away, steeling herself against that desperate need.

I'll not fall into that trap again!
****

For that instant, when her grief was at its heaviest, Liam had seen into Susa's mind. He had viewed only glimpses of exceeding hurt: visions of the cruelty done to her by Lana, Bom and ...someone else. She closed herself away too quickly for him to see who the person was who had delivered the final breaking blow, but he had gained enough to realize, she had spent considerable time as a prisoner below.

I cannot blame her for not trusting...

The knowledge gained elicited in him the emotion of protectiveness, and created a gentleness he was unaccustomed to demonstrating. He kept her wrapped close, letting her cry softly against his shoulder.

Better she let it out now, then store it, and let it fester inside.

Susa stiffened, and drew away, pretending a bravado, he knew was just a shield.

What they had mentally seen needed no discussion. Only a simple command needed giving, and she sent it by silent communiqué:

"Do not tell the humans the entryway behind has been cut off," she warned sternly.

He nodded acquiescence.

She then seemed to sense an additional dilemma, turned abruptly, and rapidly fled his presence.

****

Feather had been having difficulty with panic right from the first. As she followed Reva through the dark tunnel, her breathing became more difficult, not just because of the smoke, but because the space was so closed in. When they rounded the bend, it was better, but not by much. Now, they could stand up, but as they crossed the space where the path on one side dropped away into black nothingness, Reva seemed to vanish, as the distance between them grew farther and farther apart.

Feather would surely have become riveted to the spot in paralyzing inactivity had she not so desperately wanted outside into the fresh open air.

Until now, she had not realized she was claustrophobic.

****

Feather was rooted to the spot, unable to move, kneeling at the very edge of the empty, dark abyss, retching, gagging...nothing more was there to bring up.

She feared she was about to fall. The nausea had come upon her so suddenly, she only had time to drop to her knees, before she spewed what little she'd had to eat.

Suddenly, Susa was beside her, easing her back against the wall. Her form seemed to glow in the dark, making their surroundings dimly visible.

A bottle of water appeared in Feather's hand.

"Rinse your mouth," suggested Susa, sympathetically.

Feather obediently spit the contents on the ground.

"Drink," Susa ordered. "You'll get dehydrated."

The native girl shook her head. "It'll only come up again, later."

"Try."

The native obeyed, but just took a swallow.

Susa pushed a moist sliver of something into her other hand. Feather realized it was a section of an orange.

"Eat."

Obediently, the girl went through the motions, quite certain the food would be coming back up shortly.

Susa placed her hand gently against Feather's roiling belly, and abruptly, the nausea abated.

"I'm a diabetic," Feather explained, as if that must be the answer to her problem. "Sometimes, I can balance nature's forces, but...not down here."

"In the med bay, Zaba, the physician, implanted umbilical cord stem cells into your pancreas. It began the process of healing you of your disease. You no longer suffer from that malady."

How can I doubt anything this woman says, after all I have seen her do? It must be fact.

"Then, is it merely my fear causing this?"

"No, young one," Susa observed. "You carry..."

For a second, Feather stupidly refused to follow that thought.

No way!

"It can't be! But how?" she finally asked. "I haven't been with a man for months."

"Remember, the breeding tank?"

"Vaguely..."

113

"That's when."

Feather shivered with revulsion at the thought, her mind going back to the fuzzy images, the far away malicious, lascivious voice.

"A bit of advice," admonished Susa. "The one within you has no more blame for its conception than do you. Mother it with all the love within you. Never let it suffer for the vile deed done to you."

Feather began to softly weep. Susa enfolded her into her arms, and let the native woman cry it out. And in doing so, both realized they were gaining a friend; Feather, the mother, she had never known; Susa, the daughter, missed for so long.

They remained comforting each other, until Liam and Steven came abreast of them.

Chapter 20

Because of the heavy water tank, Steven fell behind the others, and was the last to reach the second climbing wall. He moaned audibly.

Not another balancing act! What do they think I am? It's been days since I've eaten, and my muscles are sore from being clamped to that wall for so long. Give a guy a break!

At the top, without thinking to look on the other side, he simply began to climb through. Steven caught himself only at the last minute, just before he would have fallen to his death, into a red tinted abyss.

Holy Crap! You could have warned me! What is that? Lava?

Running hundreds of miles below, was a bright molten stream, and closer up, but still yards beneath him, was what appeared to be a narrow ledge. He could see the others slowly moving along it, two by two. And running next to the wall beneath where he teetered, down to the lower ridge, was a rope ladder.

Steven backed up, out the hole again, turned around, so he could go feet first, then began the precarious climb down. He was never so relieved, as when he found that bottom rung, and his feet touched the dust-covered rock at the bottom.

****

Guilt was riding Susa. She blamed herself for the needless slaughter below. Steven, plodding behind them, reminded her of the men she had refused to help.

I should have treated them as any other captives. They were no more responsible for being down there than I was when they took me. It wasn't as if they could have escaped on their own. No matter what they chose to do, it was forced upon them; they were drugged...abused and humiliated, just as the women were.

She was not used to being constantly alert to mental invasion. Susa didn't realize Liam was reading her, that her mind was wide open, until he spoke to encourage her.

"You have saved many. How could you know Bom would sacrifice those who seemed of most value to him? Don't blame yourself..."

Quickly, she shut him out.

What right does he have to excuse me?

Then she remembered, this was Liam, not Loki.

He has no blame at all. I have been hard on him, also.

Yet, it was neither the time nor the place to discuss it.

"We need to feed our menagerie," Susa decided, using the fact to avoid the issue. "What is done; is done!" she added with bravado. "I cannot undo the past. I can only impact the present."

He nodded. "My thoughts exactly."

Susa removed her heavy backpack. Sending out a mental command to all those in the escape tunnels, she sat down against the wall.

Sit. Bread, fruit and water will come to you. As it does, pass the morsels forward until all those beyond you have had a share. I will know who hordes, and will punish. I can as easily drive you back toward the kitchens, where you will become supper for the dogs, as show you the way out of these tunnels where you are now.

She left it at that. As long as they thought it possible, most would obey, even if she was unlikely to carry out the threat.

"Harsh," Liam commented in a quiet voice, reprovingly.

She made no answer, simply began passing the food along. When her pack was empty, she realized Liam had refused to partake. Deliberately, she had done the same.

There were too many other mouths to feed.

****

Some hours later, Susa's indignant voice broke into the water carrier's vacant thoughts.

"Steven!"

Returning from some faraway mental excursion, Steven jolted to reality, becoming aware the woman was addressing him.

He still carried the full water container on his back, hadn't complained at the heavy load all through these hot tunnels, at least not aloud, but his energy was waning with every step. They had just reached a half-circle jut-in along the course.

Suddenly, Steven realized Liam had stumbled, and fallen heavily against the wall. The man seemed exhausted, in a stupor of agony, breathing heavily, sitting there, eyes closed, mouth open, panting.

The human hesitated, stood beside Susa and the giant male.

"What?"

"Unhook the water bag, and leave it. Then go to the head of the line. Tell those at the end to wait at the exit until I come. It isn't safe to just step out onto the surface."

Without objecting, Steven lowered his load. He stood there in indecision, waiting, but she turned her back, more concerned with her companion, and failed to notice.

"We need to get you out of this belt," Susa declared sympathetically to Liam.

The Noor male opened tired eyes, and searchingly studied her face. "And how do you propose to do that, without the key?"

"Let me worry on that. Be still and trust me."

His eyes wearily slid closed again.

Then to Steven's utter amazement, the normally distant woman wrapped her arms around the waist of the larger male. When there was a resounding click, she withdrew again.

Liam's eyes flew open, mirroring bewildered amazement. But he simply stared at her, saying nothing.

"Now comes the hard part," Susa admitted ruefully. "Are you ready?"

Liam grunted. "Pull away."

Steven stood just to the side of the pair, and had a perfect view of what was happening. It made him cringe when he saw what was behind, as the belt abruptly, violently pull free. On the back of the instrument were bloody, needle-like probes about a half inch thick and three inches long every six inches around its circumference. The human expected the poor man to scream, as these cruel weapons withdrew from the male's soft belly, but Liam simply pulled in a ragged breath, moaned softly in relief, and took a second painful gulp of air.

The woman dropped the gory torture belt to the side; turned toward the water barrel. A white rag just appeared in her hand. Suddenly, noticing Steven riveted to the spot, wincing in sympathy, still standing there, she demanded: "Didn't I tell you to do something?"

Steven ignored her. "He needs medical attention...a doctor."

But it was Liam who answered instead. "She knows what to do..."

Steven remained where he was, curiosity getting the better of him.

What can she possibly do for the poor guy?

"Well, if you won't do what I ask, at least make yourself useful. Tip the water sack so I can get at the water easier."

As Steven hurried forward, a basin appeared beneath the pouring spout. He tipped the soft plastic receptacle, and the tap turned on without help, the water flowing into the smaller container until it was three-quarters full, then abruptly shutting down again.

Susa touched the surface of the water in the bowl. The liquid began to steam. Quickly, she dipped the cloth in, wrung it out, and turned to the injured male.

Man! She just put her hand in boiling hot water. Is she unable to feel it, or... I wonder, how high must her body temperature be, to do that without injury?

If Susa heard his thought, she paid no attention.

"I can't do much about the broken ribs, at the moment," she said to Liam. "Not safe to heal in our present circumstances."

"Wouldn't let you," Liam declared, rebelliously.

"Oh. So, you think you could stop me?"

Liam eyed her dubiously. "Do you even know how?" he challenged. "To instant heal, I mean?"

"I didn't, until I read how from your mind," she returned with candor. "Still...the fact remains, it's unsafe to do so...down here."

Ever so slightly, he nodded.

Gently, in silence, Susa began to bathe the infected open wounds. To Steven's absolute amazement, the gaping sores began to close immediately.

"What's did you put in that water?" he asked, astounded. "That it has the power to heal like that?"

"There is nothing in it, Steven," Liam quietly disclosed. " We are self-healing. All that is needed is the touch of water to our skin."

"Holy man! Wouldn't I like to have that ability!"

"Would you also like what goes with it?" Liam demanded irritably. "To be hunted by the Roog and tortured, just for being what we are? It goes with the territory."

Steven grimaced. "No. Guess you can have it, then."

"So...now that you've witnessed your fill," Susa inquired acerbically. "Do you think you could go warn those at the end, as I asked of you before?"

Steven met her eyes with mutiny in his thoughts. He intensely disliked being ordered about by a woman. Susa held his gaze unwaveringly, not backing down. Finally, the human choosing to obey, turned and left.

****

When Steven was out of hearing, Liam asked quietly. "Why do you insist on provoking him?"

"I'm hoping he'll climb out of his funk, shed his selfish attitude, and realize he's not the only one with needs."

"He does seem to have a problem with authority," Liam agreed.

"More specific; he has a dislike of female leadership, and...prefers the submissive woman. He'd never fit into your society."

Liam couldn't help but chuckle at that.

She's an excellent judge of character.

"Still, there is good in everyone..."

"I know that...if he could just get past his prejudices. I keep hoping to incite some maturity in him. Then he'll be worth something..."

She wrung out her rag, and carefully went to bathing his wounds. After a time she spoke again.

"He needs to be paired with someone he'd hesitate to wound. Then...love might actually grow in him."

"And what might begin such a process in you?" he asked boldly. "Are you open to mating?"

"In another lifetime, I had someone..."

Abruptly, she closed her mind to him, and silently continued to work.

By that, he knew the matter was not up for discussion.

Chapter 21

Steven ran on ahead, so glad to be free of the heavy water tank, at least for the moment, that his feet seemed to have grown wings. Past the lumbering, despondent women in various stages of pregnancy; the obese naked reeking people from the meat cages.

He knew these had escape the surety of death, but it made little impression on his consciousness, other than that he was very glad he'd never been incarcerated with them.

His mind went to the woman he'd just left.

My fate could have been much worse, considering what that creature back there can do. I'd better be real careful not to get her dander up.

What makes her think she's the leader, anyway? Just because she's led us out? And why doesn't Liam challenge her? I'd rather follow him, any day! Maybe, once he's feeling better...

Reaching the end of the long ledge above the lava river, Steven drew up short, shocked by what he saw before him.

Man! Who built that? It definitely isn't natural!

At one time, Steven had been interested in cave spelunking. Though he'd never been brave enough to go on such an expedition, he had looked extensively into the information found on the internet about stalactite and stalagmite formations. These were icicle-like calcium carbonate compositions formed by the dripping of calcareous water.

The last thing he had expected was to find something like that here, where it was hot and very dry. Usually, these creations hung from the ceiling, or formed on the floor of a cavern. They were rarely horizontal across such a large expansive divide as was this bridge. It could only be manmade.

That thing must be three feet thick, and thirty feet long! It looks like a filigreed up-side-down crown that should be on a cake. And why does it glow that bright green-white color...as if it was made of tiny light filaments?

As he wondered again, who could have constructed such a thing, Susa suddenly came to mind.

Oh, I don't believe it! She couldn't have...could she?

If she can make things move without touching them, or produce objects from thin air, and clothes a naked person with a thought, why would something like this be impossible for her?

Steven shuddered, awestruck, suddenly apprehensive.

He crossed the magnificent pathway to the opposite side, where it lead into another dark corridor, all the while wondering, what was the story behind its forming.

Someday, I'll have to ask her.

****

Steven was sitting with the others, waiting in the small cavern, just beneath the fissure leading out. Above and to one side, was a large hole framed by tree roots, through which he could see moonlit sky, and twinkling stars at a distance.

He had warned the rest not to pass through; it was better to wait on the alien woman, because the giant dogs could be out there, and she alone, knew the way to where they were going. But Steven itched to set out on his own; to take his chances in the world above.

The only thing that held him back was the belief that the woman with the psychic powers could track him down, and eventually, he would pay.

Most of the time, while in this enclosed space, Steven held his breath. An overpowering stench from those around him set him to near gagging.

Even though the space was ample, and the escape aperture above allowed air in, the cavern had begun to stink. It seemed as if the meat persons had infected the pregnant and the kitchen staff with their offensive body odor, as if it had rubbed off from them to those they were helping or walked with.

Besides, at the best of times, with over a hundred people in such a confined space, perspiration from the heat alone was bound to be a problem. In the world above, according to his experience, the fat ones always had their own unique bouquet, which he had never found pleasant.

"Steven." The command did not come out loud; he merely heard a soft voice in his head. "Come back, and carry the water barrel...please."

He sighed, and rose to his feet.

Might as well. At least, I'll get away from this reeking group.

And then, a thought struck him.

Did she just say, please?

He heard a distinct chuckle in his head.

Man! There is no hiding from this woman!

He turned, and began the long trek back.

****

At the jut-out where he had left them, he found the two Noor still resting. The male looked so much better, Steven hardly recognized him as the same person. His face was free of bruising; the skin of his body smooth, the deep slashes absent. Only the slightly depressed left side of his chest evidenced the remaining unrepaired broken ribs.

Susa looked up as Steven came abreast. It was then the human realized, she wasn't looking so good herself. Her eyes had a haunted look, as if she were suffering some hidden pain of her own. And, she seemed to have aged, for when she arose, it was with stiff difficulty. She pushed herself up with her hands, first going to her knees, then shakily stood.

"Let's get going."

The packs lay side-by-side to the side of the male; one empty, the other full. The woman reached for the heavier burden.

Liam shot his hand out to stop her.

"No! My load!" he declared firmly. "You have done enough, female."

It appeared, she would challenge him, but then, thought better of it. Susa shouldered the empty rucksack, and turned to Steven.

"Water bag!" She pointed, command in her very posture.

Steven sighed.

What was the point in arguing?

But as he hefted the heavy container to his shoulders, he realized it was only half full.

Well, guess if Liam can carry a full pack with his broken ribs, I'm not so bad off carrying this.

And so the three went on again.

****

Liam had noted that Reva and Feather stayed close to Susa. He felt that was good.

At least the female has friends; they'll give her female support.

Feather acted much as a daughter would, sometimes protective, other times dependent.

Reva, on the other hand, appeared hanging on by sheer will power. He realized, she was the oldest of those they had rescued, and Liam wondered how she had managed to survive at all in the harsh environment of the prison. Now, with the heat and the darkness, the senior was flagging pitiable.

She's one feisty lady! I wonder, will she make it?

Susa must have had a similar thought, for she reached out, and gently drew the old woman to her side. Only Liam realized, that as she supported Reva, Susa gave her of her own energy.

He knew, the Noor female could not sustain healing energy to another for any long duration. But when he made to connect by touching her hand, that he might do the same for her, she pushed him away, refusing his gift.

****

When the five reached the end of the final black tunnel, and found the others waiting, Susa distributed the last of the provisions. Though each got no more than a small morsel, they were content, knowing, that was all there was.

Then they slept until day break, when Susa aroused them, saying it was safe to go above.

Chapter 22

As Thor left Universal Centre, he sent the ship into warp drive, passing through the worm hole, and coming out just at the edge of the solar system allotted to the Roog. Dropping into normal space, he let out a Feline expletive, just as Uel dropped into the seat beside him.

Thor had sent the younger male on sleep break so he would be fresh for any unexpected skirmish.

"What's the matter?" asked Uel apprehensively.

"Take a look!" growled Thor. "The dogs are airborne."

Uel looked at him uncomprehending. "I thought they always had interspace travel?"

"That's not what I refer to. They usually stay underground, unless provoked. They are cowards; prefer to stay hidden. They are headed for the outer regions, which is not normal. Something has riled them, and set them on the warpath."

Uel began to whine fearfully, and that provoked Thor's ire.

"Male! If you don't pull up your tail, and get your act together," Thor hissed angrily. "I'll leave you on the surface of that forbidden planet, at the mercy of the dogs."

Uel shrunk down into his seat, gave a whimper, and swallowed. "Don't put me back... please."

"Well, it's about time you come clean with me. I need to know what went on during Loki's stay in the prison."

Uel tried to side track. "How we going to get passed the dog ships?"

"Let me worry about that. I'll go in cloaked; hide behind the moon of the third planet for a while...until we are safe to go to Liam."

"Maybe...he's escaped, and that's what all the fuss is about?"

"If he has, good! But, the dog ships are equipped for war. They wouldn't be, if they were simply looking for one Noor."

Much to Thor's frustration, Uel held his silence the entire time it took for the older male to move the invisible ship through the multitude of Roog carriers at the perimeter of the system. Once safely past the outer planets, Thor maneuvered his shuttle to the dark side of the moon circling the third planet.

Then, putting the controls on auto, he spun his chair to face the cowering younger member.

"Now! You will tell me what it is you are hiding. Do I need to scruff you, male?"

Uel whined, and covered his head with his paws.

"What is it with you? Are you friend or foe to the Noor?"

"I am loyal..."

"Then, why do you refuse to disclose what is detrimental to the Junction pair?"

"Because...Loki said..."

"To keep quiet?" finished Thor. "Why? Why would he think that necessary?"

"Bom..."

"Bom what? He threatened retribution? Look around. It's already coming. And it's not the first time we've been under his vindictive eye. I need to know what we are up against! Tell me; what happened down there."

"I don't know it all," pleaded Uel.

"Then tell me what you do know."

Uel swallowed. "Bom tortured Loki. It was rumored he killed him...then Loki...somehow, came back."

"Yeah. No doubt because the two males were not together."

Uel's jaw dropped. "They are safe apart?"

"Why do you think they separate? It gives them an edge. Now, is there something else I should know? Why is there such a rift between the two?"

"I don't know about that..."

"Okay. Back to in prison. There's something else, isn't there?"

Uel wouldn't meet his eyes.

"I guess you'd rather see the Noor species die..."

"No," whined Uel.

"Okay; then spill it!"

"There was a female..."

Thor laughed, despite himself. "Go on."

"I don't know exactly what happened, but...she was human, and...Loki healed her, and...she had powers after...like a Noor..."

"Ha! The missing one! It all makes sense, now. What became of her?"

"I think, somehow, Loki set her free. Bom was real mad!"

"This gets better and better. So, Loki's staying quiet, so she is kept safe. Are you aware of why Liam went to the Forbidden planet?"

Uel shrugged.

"He went looking for this lost one."

"Ohhh..." hissed Uel in consternation.

"And, I just bet, he found her!" Thor concluded to himself. "One more question."

Thor studied the other intently, to watch for any deception.

"Was Loki intimate?"

Uel's pupils went to large horror filled pools. The scent of guilt was oozing from every pore.

"What was your part in this, male?" Thor growled. "You trick him? And, as with any true Noor, he returned the favor by freeing you," he added sarcastically.

"Well...you'll live with that guilt the rest of your days."

He pounded Uel's thigh energetically, causing the male to wince from the blow.

"But...don't worry. I'll keep this to myself while things play out. In circumstances such as these, silent observation is always the best method. We are guardians to the Noor children, and we, will be the ones to help them find their place in the universe."

"Now," Thor hissed, as an afterthought. "The question is, are you willing to die for the Junction pair?"

A small whimper of fear passed through the young male, then he sat up stiffly to full stature, and, with all the courage he could muster, declared:

"Yes! Sir! For Loki!"

"To guard the one, is to protect both. They are one entity."

Chapter 23

They had just stepped out on the surface, when Susa directed the long line of escapees, to start out for the tree line in the distance without her. She had also allotted the empty water sack, and packs, to men from the kitchen, which suited Steven just fine.

Only two women, Feather and Reva, remained behind to watch with their benefactor. Susa sat down to the side, busying herself with the old torture belt, that the larger imprisoned male had worn.

Steven wasn't interested in what she was doing; his eyes were on the giant; who was fast becoming his idol. The Noor male stood, arms raised, reaching for the sun, as if the rays had the power to heal him.

As the human watched, the concaved side of Liam's chest seemed to expand. He took a deep painless breath, as if the ribs beneath were no longer a problem.

Don't tell me the sun heals them, too?

"It does," answered Liam, as if Steven had spoken aloud.

As the male turned toward him, he was suddenly clothed with loose fitting leggings and a long-sleeve sweat shirt in a light shade of blue.

"Oh, man! You can thought read too," exclaimed the human man in consternation. "Man! How's a guy get any privacy from you...whatever you are?"

"I am Noor...part feline, as well. And as for blocking from us, I only read, if necessary."

"What is she?" Steven asked, nodding in the direction of the mentally dexterous female.

"From what I can judge...she's a mix of human, Feline, and Noor."

"Oh. Say...you couldn't make me some clothes, could you? Down below, I had to be like this, but...a guy feels a bit exposed up here."

Liam chuckled. "And, what would you like?"

"Maybe...some jeans would be good. And...a leather jacket. Ah...and a shirt."

At each word he spoke, the apparel appeared on his person.

"Ah...how about some shoes...or boots."

"No need for footwear. The climate is still mild."

Liam turned back, and lifted his face to the sun again. It was then Steven noted, his feet were unshod, as well.

Guess, I'll have to be satisfied with what I can get.

After a time, Liam again faced Steven; spoke quietly. "Are you not going to join the others, male?"

"Figure it's safest right here."

"You think so, do you? A Noor can fry your brain, should it so desire..."

Steven's jaw dropped. "Males, too?"

Liam laughed. "Until now, I was in a belt; it kept my powers dormant. In the dark, I could not re-energize, but now, in the light, I am at full strength...and yes, males have powers, also."

"Just what is a Noor?"

"I'll let you discover that on your own. Noor means light, we stand for good..."

"Okay then. Still say, I'm safest here...you'd protect me, right?"

Liam hissed. "Oh, human." He shook his head as if disappointed. "Well, you are indeed right; it is to your best interest to stay with us. The surface here will never be the same. Shortly, it will be broiling with Roog predators...they will no longer be herders. From now on, they will hunt above ground, and no human will be safe. Sticking with us is definitely your best option."

Steven didn't like the sound of that.

Hesitating only slightly, Liam went on: "I am in need of someone to watch my back. Do you think, human, you could come out of your self-absorbency long enough to defend another if needed?"

Steven was taken aback.

Self-absorbed? Me?

Liam grunted, as if he was reading him again.

"You mean, you need protection against the woman?"

Liam growled in frustration.

Why the devil is he mad at me? That female's really gotten under his skin. I can relate to that.

Liam hissed angrily.

"And...if...you do...serve me, I will expect you to give Susa respect, or...I will have to deal with you!"

It galled Steven, the man had the nerve to assume he'd just fall into line.

"Who says, I want to be a servant? I'll do it for wages, but not as your slave." At Liam's glower of warning, Steven chose the path of less resistance. "A man's got to eat you know... What's say?"

His pretended bravado got him nowhere.

"In my world, where you will be going, a male is either a treasured guardian, or a non-descript warrior. Perhaps, you'd like to fight on the front lines?"

"How much does that pay?"

Somberly, Liam answered. "For both stations, all necessities are freely provided."

"You mean, free?" Liam nodded. "Food? Clothing? What about spending money?"

"What need is there of currency? All you need is provided: medical care, entertainment, all of what you formally mentioned, at no cost. You merely need to serve five eight hour shifts."

"But...I don't get paid?"

"We don't buy loyalty! Decide now! You can go on your way, or...take your chances as my defender."

"Well...not sure I'll be much protection," Steven finally admitted. "You're the guy with the powers..."

Liam hissed, frustrated. "We have our weaknesses. But if you can't be trusted, you'll only betray me. Then, you might as well go on your way. If you continue to follow me, I'll consider that as consent."

****

With the modified belt in hand, Susa approached the two men. As she had been working, she blocked out their conversation, but she had the gist of what Liam had offered the human. She would deal with that last.

When she handed the power belt to Liam, he frowned. "What's this?"

"Put it on. I've done the same to it, as with the one I wear."

He dropped to his knees, sat back on his heels, turning over the instrument in his hands in wonder.

"It stores extra energy...and mimics the drain belt reaction? We don't lose the energy drained; it holds it instead? Incredible! How did you come up with this idea?"

"Desperate need, and...time under Bom..."

"But...I thought only I had..."

"Know you not, your exceptional skills must have a duplicate in a female? Such has nature prepared it...as a balance. Now, for your own safety, please put it on...that is, if you intend to stay on the surface?"

"I will not be leaving the planet until I have fulfilled my mission." Rising, he snapped the belt around his middle.

"Are you certain, Bom can be fooled a second time?"

"Should you be recaptured, it would first be by an underling. If he has a wand, and uses it on us, the only vulnerability will be just after it is done. We will both need to be alert..."

"And it would be a help, if we had friends around us to fight the beasts, while the belt goes its cycle."

Susa nodded, turning to Steven standing nearby.

"What of this one?"

"If he chooses to remain with us, I'll take responsibility for him."

"You'll keep him in line?"

"If he seeks his own self-preservation, it is my risk, but, as for respect, and the risking of the group, if he shirks, I will discipline."

Susa hissed in skepticism, then gave Steven a warning.

"If you care...there is a ten minute recovery delay, after he's hit with a drain beam, and goes down."

"That's shorter than yours..." Liam noted.

"Mine is the same, but Bom had his weapon set to kill a Noor."

"How did you come back, then? You should be dead; you are a physical?"

"Both."

"But, how came you back?" Liam demanded a second time.

"That secret, I will keep to myself. See that this male is not a detriment to us."

"I got ears, and I ain't some commodity," Steven cut in.

"You heard me, Liam," Susa admonished, turning from the two.

"I don't take lip from no woman!" Steven shouted after her.

And Susa heard the Noor male hiss at the human. "It is not the time to put up a fight. Cut your losses, while you're ahead!"

Chapter 24

As they walked through the trees, Liam watched his companion's mind, hoping she would let him in, but she always kept locked away. He did, however, note her mental exterior activity.

"You keep the group shielded," he observed.

"They need protection; don't they?"

Liam extended his outer awareness. He had been so intent on the female, he'd not realized their danger. She also raised the screen slightly, from misty fog to transparency.

Beside Susa, Reva began to keen softly in fear, for now the humans could see what lay in the shadows. The giant Rottweiler-like Roog were all around them, hunting like a pack of wolves.

"Quiet, Reva," Susa cautioned gently. "They may still be able to hear."

"I can put up a sound barrier," Liam suggested.

"Don't need your help," Susa declared stubbornly. "We need to get the humans to the river to wash. The dogs scent the meat persons."

"I could created a delusion; send them off a different way."

"Some will still follow this trail..."

"For mercy sake, don't be so intent on doing all yourself," Liam reproved. "The best leader is one who delegates."

"Do it, then!"

****

Liam sent out the powerful delusion to the minds of the Roog, a scent illusion powerfully strong, leading away from the river, in the opposite direction from where the large party of humans were headed. It would force the dogs back to the field from which the escapees had come.

At first their predators seemed confused, milling uncertainly, but finally, their leader headed off, away, and most of the rest began dropping back, finally following, until only one or two remained. Those few were determined they were not mistaken; the quarry was beside them. At last, they too gave up.

Liam had also successfully masked the odor of the humans from the dogs.

All through these goings on, Steven had watched his Noor companion intently, as if he expected to see an outward sign of what Liam was doing, like smoke issuing from his ears, or face contortions. Liam almost laughed, at the thoughts going through the human's mind.

As the two trudged along at the end of the line, it seemed, Steven could hold his peace no longer.

"You made them smell something else?" he wished to know. "So, does that mean, you can trick any mind...of other creatures, I mean, into seeing or believing what isn't there?"

"I told you previously, if a Noor wished, he could direct you to take your own life, or fry that limited intelligence, you are so proud of. Just know this, we are benevolent. It isn't in our usual nature to harm another."

"But...if that woman ordered you to, you'd kill, wouldn't you?"

Liam let that one slide. It wasn't worth getting into.

"Both the races I belong to are led by females. In the Noor past, we had a mighty queen... with the most powerful of minds, far greater than any of the then known males..."

Steven digested that for a moment, then bluntly asked. "What happened to her?"

"In the end, some lost their respectful mind-set...they chose to withhold honor from the Queen. When it was most needed, those males failed to protect her adequately, and all of the pure race was lost because of it."

"Bummer!" was all the human had to say. "Guess, you all learned that lesson the hard way."

Liam wanted to hit him.

What will it take, human, for you to learn that lesson?

Liam shook himself, barely able to restrain his anger.

Why do I even bother? It's as if I am compelled to mentor this ignorant human.

****

It was near dusk, when Liam came to the river with the last of the stragglers. Most of the humans were now bathed, and were seated in groups waiting to go on. Susa stood back near the tree line watching, still in protection mode.

"Why don't you bathe while you have a chance?" Susa suggested, when Liam joined her.

"I think, I prefer a more private setting," Liam declared. "I'll wait until we arrive at where we are headed."

"If you think you'll get a pleasant pool for your pleasure, think again. The men bathe in the river at our settlement."

Liam sighed. "I did not mean to appear to want privilege. Why don't you bathe? I'm sure, by now, you must have great need. I can maintain an adequate shield protection in your place."

"No, thank you. I'll wait for home. Too many males around."

He chuckled. "If you cannot trust that I would prevent an assault on your person, at least depend on your Maker to..."

He stopped short, as he got a flash of memory she sent him: inside the prison, many naked women, dancing in agony, as scalding jets of hot medicated water sprayed them from all sides.

"Oh, hell!" Liam clamped his mind down; turned away, unable to handle what he'd seen.

What the devil has she been through? Bom, what unmitigated evil have you been up to?

Immediately, she called to the others, and started them through the forest again.

"What did she do to you?" asked Steven curiously.

"She sent me a memory..."

"Of what?"

"I believe, it was of the Roog shower technique for..."

"The cattle?"

"Damn it, human. Are you so insensitive? I suppose, you've seen it?"

"No, but I've heard about the method they use for the breeders."

"Spit! Spit!" hissed Liam, moving away. "Let's get out of here. It'll be dark soon."

****

Liam was now striding beside Susa, and her two shadow companions, Reva and Feather. And Steven kept pace with Liam. Both Noor were ignoring their human companions.

The giant male tried once more to break the icy barrier between them.

"What is the real reason you won't trust me?" he asked, coming right to the point. "Show me the problem, and I'll try to rectify it."

Still, she kept her mind closed to him, giving no reply. Perturbed, he tried a different angle.

"Do you have a belief in an Almighty Creator?"

That finally got a reaction. Susa screwed up her face in a wary grimace.

"Sometimes, it seems like God has forsaken me."

Using her own vernacular; using the male pronoun, he made an effort to comfort.

"We often expect instant aid. He protects, and we fail to notice. His timing is idyllic. He watches, waits for the perfect moment, teaches us through the process."

"Waits too long for some...like Lana."

Liam chose to ignore that tragic memory, went on, preferring not to dwell, or be deterred.

"We have this Noor belief: nothing happens by chance. You yourself said, 'Lana's actions were a benefit in the end'."

Susa groaned at being parried with her own words. Otherwise, she remained silent, giving him the chance to voice his opinion.

"The Almighty Creator guides each step. But...sometimes, when we make mistakes, we often have to pay a price..."

"You are saying, all these are being punished?"

"No. Only learning the hard way."

Suddenly, she was angry.

"What of the innocent? Many people on Earth have gone the way of evil: rape, murder, child abuse...molesters. Always, the perpetrators are allowed their rights; but the victims are never spoken for...and, while you are at it, don't forget, that dog breed. Did God create their blood lust?"

She had struck a note dear to Liam's heart. His underlying pet disagreement with the ruling Universal counsel was this very issue.

"Such diabolical existences, both human and Roog, are not of the Almighty's making! I can only speak of the situation I am familiar with: the dog threat came about because our ruling council gave the Roog free reign, and the right to appease their carnal appetites in this solar system, without being policed. It was in error! And it will stop! When I report what I have seen. Out in the universe, the Almighty does rule! But...in the meantime, like you say, those here pay the price."

"Oh, so much power you think you have, male," Susa challenged. "How much can one minor being do? Very little!"

Oh, bother! Reality check here. How right she is.

Liam suddenly realized, he'd not only revealed more of his feelings than he had meant to, but he'd gotten sidetracked from his original purpose. He'd intended to comfort, and placate, and in his frustration gotten nowhere.

"I am sorry. Forgive. Noor should be peaceable, but perhaps...my Feline nature got the upper hand."

He had the uncomfortable feeling he was repeating something unpleasant she had experience from another, for she tensed, and went silent. Her quiet became uncomfortable, and Liam wondered what more he might say.

"I believe," she finally declared, returning to their former discussion. "God wishes us to help others, as much as we are able. He did not give me these new talents to gratify my own desires alone..."

"Exceedingly commendable," Liam agreed. "I have come to that conclusion, as well, but... together we would be so much more effective...Why won't you trust me?"

She cut him down quickly."

"I have learned I cannot put my trust in most men...especially a Noor male."

Liam stopped walking. Frowned.

"When have I given you reason to mistrust me?"

"You...have not...yet! But you will."

She moved away quickly, thrusting ahead, making it obvious, she wished no further discussion, and would rather be alone.

Chapter 25

Reva had hurried to keep pace with Susa. No matter what these men might think, or how they acted toward the alien woman, the older woman realized, there was more to Susa, than the outer attitude of man-hate, she projected. Inside this girl was a wounded soul, battered, perhaps by other men, but definitely hurting, with no trustable friend at her disposal... at least, not among those with her at present.

So Reva simply stayed at her side, as if to let Susa know, as Reva had received, now she was willing to give; silent, supportive, and sympathetic, though the elder had no inkling of what drove the self-destruction.

After a time, as Reva watched Susa in side profile, she observed the unchecked tears. Everyone else was so intent on their own misery, expecting leadership from this woman, they failed even to notice.

Susa marched at the head of the line, stoic to the eyes of the others, yet obviously, fighting her own demons. As tears betray her, she would brush them away each time, hold her breath a moment, steeling herself for another step forward, and continue on.

It was when the woman stopped doing that, Reva began to worry.

Gradually, it seemed, Susa detached, went to some place distant, as if her mind had had too much.

Fear flooded over Reva, when she noticed the opaque shielding around the group slowly dissipating.

Something is very wrong. Maybe, I should warn the male?

****

Liam and Steven were back in the middle of the line, as it meandered through the trees. By this time, each man carried one of the pregnant women, who had reached the point of near collapse, and been swooped up, first by Liam; then in obedience, as directed, the second, by Steven.

Liam suddenly stopped dead in his tracks, causing his human companion behind, to nearly collide with his back. But the Noor was not concerned with what was happening at his rear. His mind was reaching out toward the female at the head of the line.

He could feel confusion, and though her mind was still shielded from him, he sensed extreme befuddlement. Liam was acquainted with the condition. Back home, Twila, his foster sister, was especially prone to this. Susa, up ahead, had reached the point of physical exhaustion, and her mind had shut down; she was about to pass out.

"What's wrong?" asked Steven. But Liam ignored him.

Abruptly, and without ceremony, Liam set his burden down, and took off at a run.

****

Remembering his duty toward the Noor male, trusting his judgments to be unflawed, Steven set his charge on her feet, and sped after Liam.

****

Liam was twenty feet from Susa, when he saw her begin to fall. He sped up, becoming as a mere blur, as he travelled past the shambling humans.

Susa stopped, knees buckling, folding like a flaccid rag doll toward the ground. Liam reached her side, just before she hit, scooping her into his arms. Then he continued, at the head of the line, as if nothing had happened, her limp unconscious form resting against his shoulder, as if it were the most natural of conditions.

And Liam felt his own body tingling with pleasure, not simply in pride at accomplishing the perfect save, but at the touch of, what he now knew, was...his female.

****

Coming abreast of Liam, his breath labored, Steven demanded in alarm:

"What's wrong with her?"

Liam hissed at him ferociously, reminiscent of a jungle cat defending its kill, as if this was his mate, and he would do anything to protect.

"Well, don't throw a hissy fit. I didn't do anything to her."

Liam growled low in his throat, and then seemed to adjust his attitude to a more civilized tone, at last including Steven.

"She's reached her limit," he vaguely informed.

"Is she dangerous?"

"Not to a selfish human!" the male answered curtly.

For once, it dawned on Steven, he was being callous.

"Sorry," he acknowledged quietly. It was unlike Steven to ever apologized. "Didn't mean it like it sounds." After a moment, he added: "The shield is down."

"I am aware," Liam declared brusquely. "I have more important things to worry on. All are reasonably safe, for the moment. Perhaps, this is a time to watch out for others?"

"Me?"

"Yes, you."

"How?"

"Warn if you hear, see, or even smell, enemy..." Liam suggested. "And be prepared to do battle..."

"With my bare hands?"

Liam hissed in frustration. "Are you unable to think on your own, human? I was under the impression your kind was intelligent." After a second, he came back with a suggestion, in a less argumentative tone. "Sticks are weapons..."

Shamed, Steven searched the ground at their feet, and came up with a sizable club.

But, how much can one man do against the giant Roog?

Then it occurred to him.

"Find yourself weapons!" he shouted to those around them.

Behind his back, Steven failed to see a slight smile fleetingly cross Liam's face.

****

At the head of the bedraggled group, Liam halted again. Suddenly, he and Steven were surrounded by an advance of human sentries. Steven raised his club menacingly, but Liam sent him a thought warning.

They are friend.

When the weapon was lowered, a black male stepped forward, his manner one of threat.

"What have you done to Susa?" Norris demanded. "Who are you, Noor?"

"I am, Liam. I was in the prison; she rescued me..."

The dark man took a moment to think on the circumstances.

Liam added incentive. "She was exhausted...collapsed."

Norris moved closer; grunted; chose to trust. "Okay. She needs water. I've seen her like this before. Follow me."

He gave orders to the other sentries to guard the perimeter, then turned, and led them in; Liam, carrying the still unconscious Susa, following close behind. Steven joined them; Feather and Reva hurried to keep up. And behind, the guards let through a constant stream of humans, as if they had been expected.

****

Liam stepped over the joist of the door frame, into the kitchen of a large log cabin. A plump Caucasian woman, in her mid seventies, turned from the sink, as her thinner partner preceded the Noor.

"Huh! Norris! They are here at last?"

"Susa's in a bad way, Downy," Norris revealed to his wife. "I think she's been using her powers too much again. You know what to do for her better than I..."

"Water," agreed the woman. "Bring her..."

As Liam followed, bearing Susa, he heard the Black man order those behind to stay where they were. This couple seemed to be the ones in charge.

In a large community bath/shower room, Downy turned to face him.

"Prop her up against the wall in one of the stalls..."

Liam obliged, stepped back. He longed for water himself, but he would not put his needs or wants before those of a female.

"I can take care of her. I've seen her naked before..."

Downy cut him off. "I'm sure you have, mister," she affirmed indignantly. "But I am a woman; you are a man, and Susa deserves privacy. I can take care of her. Now, turn around, get out of here, and shut the door, as you go out."

She stood with hands on hips, awaiting his obedience, expecting it. Liam knew, this was not the time to argue.

Chapter 26

Liam had refused to leave the structure until he was certain Susa was up again. With mental sight, he'd kept track of things, being discrete, but aware of what transpired beyond the closed door.

This, they cannot prevent!

The humans seemed unaware of his abilities, as if Susa had kept her telepathic talents a secret. He would, also, if that were for the best. Only Steven knew of them, and perhaps the two women shadows, Susa had picked up.

Feather and Reva had been integrated into the household without question. Remarkably, Steven had remained at Liam's side. And most of the inhabitants, simply ignored the two men.

When Liam was satisfied Susa was conscious, and had been led to a room to sleep, he sat down at the closest wall to her chamber, and finally, relaxed. Steven did likewise. The two were brought food and water. At last, Liam dozed off.

Now it was mid afternoon of the next day, and the Noor male paced the floor of the large living room like a restless tom cat, waiting impatiently. He sensed, Susa had just woken up.

Just as the female put in an appearance, Downy peeked her head around the doorjamb of the kitchen.

"Well, that's a sight for sore eyes. Ready for some lunch?"

Liam stepped forward, as if to speak, but Susa waved him away, annoyed. Instead, she addressed the woman from the kitchen.

"Anything I need to deal with?"

"Well?" Downy pondered on the request. "Oh, yes! We need garments for the new pregnant ones. Some of them are already too large for what we have on hand, and...males also need something to wear."

"Done. I've just placed all you need in the far storage."

"Thank you. Also," said Downy. "We've had a problem with two of the men who insist on fighting..."

"I'll see to their discipline..."

"Not before you eat first, girl," objected the older woman.

Susa disagreed. "I'll have something from the garden, where I will be monitoring the enforcement of their punishment."

Downy laughed. "Good to have you back, dear. Since you left, it's been like policing a preschool."

As Susa passed through the outer door, Downy added: "One of the new ones will deliver in the next couple hours..."

Susa shot back over her shoulder: "Call me, if there are complications, and you need help."

****

As she left the cabin, Liam, with Steven at his back, was right behind Susa. Out in the yard, she spun on them, hissing like a cornered tigress.

"Don't follow me!" she growled at Liam. "I don't need your protection! Go take a bath; you still reek of the prison."

She turned on Steven, venomously.

"And you! I've had enough of you, too! You want to live here with us, you work! In the garden...better still, here's a job for you. You are so anxious to protect someone? Try this! Amara needs help with her baby; the little one is teething. She, needs a guardian, more than Liam!"

Steven bristled visibly.

"I'm no nursemaid..."

Her angry hiss cut him off, and had the man stepping back.

"You...will...protect...her! And if any harm comes to her, by your hand, or any other, I will personally take your life! Do you understand?"

In Steven's mind, he had no doubt that this female could kill him, but Liam knew, Noor females did not have it in them to wantonly take another's life, though the idea did pass across his mind, that in grief, or desperate circumstance, Susa might lose control.

She whirled on him, obviously reading, incensed by his mental musing.

"Get from me, male! I don't want you!" she thundered. "I don't want to see your face again until..."

Liam sent her a visual feeling of a kind, gentle, comforting hug, meant to appease her. For a second her eyes brimmed with welling tears, as her need for such a concerned embrace near broke her, then abruptly, the emotion was conquered, closed away, and replaced by a quiet stoic control.

"I don't need you," she moan-whispered, half under her breath. Turning, she strode wearily away, toward the seclusion of the garden.

Liam knew beyond a doubt, though she denied it so intensely, Susa more than needed his care and love. And being raised a guardian in the Feline world, he'd not leave her in that disadvantaged condition, if he could help it.

But, for the moment, it was best to do as she said.

****

As they made for the river, Steven was seething with anger.

That woman! Who put her in command? And Liam...why is he such a milksop?

"Why do you put up with her?" he challenged. "You're big enough to put that little bitch in her place..."

The words were hardly out of his mouth, when Liam turned snarling. The Noor had to be over eight feet tall, and though not of chunky build, must weigh in at over five hundred pounds.

Suddenly, Steven was swinging in midair, suspended by the back of his leather jacket. The human exceeded six feet, and ranged near two hundred and thirty pounds, himself, but in the fist of the giant Noor, he both looked like, and felt, as a wayward kitten being punished, dangling there above the ground.

The male shook Steven violently. His visual perception dimmed, and swam dizzily; his teeth jarred against each other.

"If ever I hear disrespect toward Susa from you again, I'll break every bone in your body, do you hear?" Liam growled in his ear.

Steven had no doubt, Liam could and would do what he said, and inwardly, the human man was terrified, but his own temper had not yet cooled.

"I could just leave," he fired back rebelliously.

With jarring swiftness, Liam set him on his feet.

"Go for it!" Liam dared. "I've about had enough of you, human. Go!" With his hand he made a gesture, as if to shoo him away. "But remember this, the Roog still prowl about, and they look for those who were stolen from them..."

Steven's courage fled, as did the remnants of his displeasure. He quickly realized, his chances were next to nil on his own.

Liam turned without another word, heading for the water. Steven followed after, meek now, and compliant.

****

When the two men entered the gardens after bathing, Liam was shocked by what he found. He had expected a small, simple vegetable plot, behind the hedge.

At first glance, from the outside, the space appeared quite small, but when entering the barrier, it was like stepping into another dimension. It was as if space had been bent, stretched, and expanded.

This was on a measure equal to anything aboard his foster mother Dia's ship, which had vast, long established, hydroponics networks, but rather than in the bowels of an enormous metal space craft, it was outdoors.

Here were fields of corn, oats and wheat, fruit trees of all kinds, and large vegetable plots, stretching for half a mile, while out on the far horizon were barns housing chickens, pigs, and milk cows with calves. Dotted about among the trees and plants were the industrious workers.

At the perimeter, surrounding all of this, grew thorn hedges, intertwined to create an impenetrable barricade, with the only access, through the gate by the house.

At the far end, in a gap, where a section was still unfinished, two men, with the aid of sticks, were attempting to force the injurious trees to interlace. They wore leather protective body coverings and head gear, but despite these, the thorns found penetration, and blood was evident, where they often had found their mark.

The trees grew to a height of over eight feet, so that at times the men would need a stepladder to complete their task. As they finished with one tree, a new bush would miraculously grow, filling in the next empty section beside it. So also, the ladder disappeared or reappeared when needed.

Seated against the trunk of a fruit tree nearby, was Susa, eating an apple. It was obvious, it was she who supplied, and supervised the men.

As Liam and Steven approached, the man on the ladder, reach too far over, and fell into the lethal obstacle. He would have been torn to pieces, but suddenly, without explanation, he was again on his feet, righted, and at a safe distance.

Liam was not surprised.

I knew she did not have it in her to harm another!

The worker turned pleadingly to the Noor female.

"Please, Susa, we'll be good. I won't fight any more. I promise."

"Complete the barrier," she ordered quietly, not yielding, her tone seemingly unconcerned.

The man turned back, and again climbed the ladder.

Liam almost chuckled aloud.

I'll have to remember this one in regards to Steven. It is most effective.

"What do you want?" Susa growled, noticing them.

Liam's smile fled. He still had a far ways to gain her good graces.

"Where do you want us to work?" he asked meekly.

"Well. You can have your pick. There are barns that constantly need to be mucked out, and fruit to be picked...it is always harvest..."

Liam looked at the trees about them. They were unlike the usual orchard trees of a planet. It seemed they were both in flower and fruit at the same time.

How did she do that? Where did she ever see such a thing?

"I got the idea from the bible...in Revelation," Susa answered, matter-of-fact. "Well? What will it be?"

"We'll do fruit," Liam decided.

"You'll find what you need beneath the trees over there." She pointed at a nearby shed with wooden barrels beside it, and soft sacks thrown over them. "Take the full tubs in to Downy..."

He knew by that, they had been summarily dismissed.

Chapter 27

At Liam's insistence, Steven went in search of Amara. He'd been told, she was the only one with a small child. He found her in the living room, nursing the baby.

Steven had seen her around the night before, but without the infant. She wasn't much to look at, dark hair and eyes; slim and not too tall; would easily fit beneath his arm. She appeared to be in her late teens, but when she shyly met your eyes, which was rare, the dark shields were filled with hidden tragedy and aged experience.

She didn't seem old enough to have an infant, and he blurted the question without thinking.

"How old are you, anyway?"

She looked up at him, not the least bit taken aback. "Susa says, I am actually twenty-five..."

And of course, Susa is always right.

He'd let that one go for now.

Steven sat down on the chesterfield beside Amara.

Before his capture, it was his custom to either enamor himself to a woman to fill his needs, or visit scorn and derision upon those who had wronged him. But, with this woman, he did not feel the usual animosity. Somehow, it seemed harder to be angry at her; she was not to blame, for the fact her care had been forced upon him.

"I was told, I'm to help you..."

"I could sure use it." She sighed with relief.

When the infant ceased to suckle, she moved the small girl to her knee. The baby whined fretfully, as if not yet satisfied.

"Will you hold her a while? I need a bathroom break."

Amara didn't wait for a reply, simply transferred the little one to him, and rose to leave.

Caught off guard, Steven hadn't expected that. He had never had much to do with children. The doctors had told him, his swimmers were lazy, that it would take a miracle for him to father a child. For a long time, he had longed for a boy to carry on his name. Finally, he had accepted the fact, he'd be the last of his line, and gone on with life.

Now, Steven felt extreme panic. He held the baby balanced on his knee, at arm's length.

It was the tiny girl who broke the ice. She suddenly found his nose, and Steven forgot all about the fact, the mother had stepped from the room, leaving them alone.

****

When Amara returned, Steven and baby were playing 'name the parts'. He hadn't expected such a young child to have a vocabulary, but she knew the words, when he voiced them, and repeated each in her own way.

Amara took a seat beside them, and quietly watched.

Quite unexpectedly, the child abruptly stopped playing, cuddled against Steven's shoulder and began to suck her thumb. So suddenly did she fall asleep, Steven thought something was wrong.

"Is she sick?" he asked in alarm.

Amara chuckled softly. "Oh, no. With Susa gone so long, and her teething without help, she hasn't slept much..."

Steven was puzzled, wondering why it made a difference that Susa wasn't there. In answer to his questioning look, Amara explain further.

"Susa's like a grandmother to her. She's preferred the Noor, since she was born, and somehow...Susa helps my little girl with the pain of colic, when we are unable...If you want, I can take her."

"Naw, she's comfortable. If we moved her, it would probably just wake her."

So Amara sat beside him, resting her head against the back of the couch. She looked so weary herself, as if she too could just drop off.

"Does the baby have a name?" Steven asked after a time.

"We all just call her TaTa. For some reason, that's what she calls herself."

"TaTa." Steven chuckled softly. "It suits her."

Silence reigned for a time. Steven was struggling with questions he wanted to ask, but could find no way to phrase them, so they would not offend.

"Why does everyone treat Susa, as if she was some sort of god?"

Catching his drift immediately, despite his attempt to hide it, Amara sat up, her back erect, instantly indignant and offended.

"Without Susa, none of us would be alive! We were her first. She came back for me especially...me and another. She did not have to, and...she could have much more easily have escaped without us..."

And then came a story Steven had never expected. Though he knew all the facets of Bom's prison, Steven had never connected those inside, that abominable life, with the people of this sanctuary. It had never dawned on him, there had been a first attempt.

As the tale poured from Amara's lips, he realized the tunnel they had passed through had been formed at the expense of the Noor female's own health, and much tragedy, loss, and tears, had accompanied their passage through it.

He could easily visualize and empathize, as Amara spoke of the conditions of the fleeing party. When the woman recounted the death of Beth, the failed attempt to save her, the devastation to the woman who had given it her all, he felt an almost guilty, as if he had been responsible for the death of the poor teen.

As the story teller switched to the birth of TaTa, he cringed in abject horror, living it all with the mother. He had never known these Noor could be so sacrificial, and no more, could he fault any for their deeds.

Steven's image of Susa had changed with the telling. He was appalled at his behavior. No wonder this miniature woman beside him, all those here worshiped the Noor female. They had gone through hell together.

At last, too spent to speak of the circumstances any longer, Amara leaned back and closed her eyes. She sighed, exhausted, moved over against him, rested her head against his shoulder. Soon, her even breathing told him, she had fallen asleep.

For the next hour, Steven sat there undisturbed, one arm about Amara, the other cuddling the baby that had been born in the dungeons. And somewhere, during the course of his thoughts, he began thinking of them as his family.

****

It was very early the next morning. Amara was pacing the floor with a screaming TaTa, and Steven was trying desperately to distract the teething, hurting infant, before she woke the whole household. Liam had already been aroused, but though the Noor male thought he could help, the baby would not let him near.

"Sus...Sus," begged the tortured child, huge tears spilling down her swollen cheeks. She let out a shriek of unbridled misery, near deafening those around them.

And suddenly, Susa was beside them, gathering the sobbing infant to her breast, her temper evident, as well, as if she had absorbed the fear, frustration, and upset of the suffering one.

"Go! Go!" she ordered angrily. "Leave me alone with her!"

When the three hesitated, Susa exploded with wrath.

"Get out of here! Go to the gardens! Make yourselves useful!"

Prudently, Liam began to move the others toward the door. But, though Steven reluctantly obeyed, his ever present temper had surfaced again, and the Noor female was the target. He was steaming, but wisely held his peace, for the sake of the child.

****

Steven didn't wait for her to speak. As soon as Susa stepped into the garden without TaTa, he was at her.

"You sure think you're the queen of the universe, don't you?"

Liam turned from the raspberry bush he was picking at, to watch the argument, almost chuckling, but Steven saw his grin, and turned on him.

"What's so funny, you big cat?" Steven challenged bitterly.

Liam's eyes narrowed in sudden annoyance, not just at being drawn into the disagreement, but more at the derogatory implication.

"I am not a cat!" he growled in return. "I am Feline/Noor! A cat is a primitive!"

"Oh, soor...ry," Steven fired back acerbically. "Seems you are just as high and mighty as this she is."

"You wanted to know, what is so funny? Fool! This she, you refer to, is meant to be the Universal Queen, the leader of the Noor peoples..."

Steven blinked. "What?" he asked in a more civil, subdued tone. "How...how'd that happen?"

Before Liam could say more, Susa cut in. "That will be enough, male!" she curtly commanded, in a hushed, barely controlled voice. "If that were true, I would not want such a station..."

Liam decided to argue the point. "You hold the Essence. You may seek to remain in obscurity, hidden here among humans, but the fact remains, you are what you are. You will someday rule us."

"From now on, you will keep that to yourself...until the knowledge is needed," she returned quietly. "Please."

"Is that a command, my Lady?"

Her temper flared. "Seeing as you are the wise one, and I see, little can be hidden from your expansive intelligence, you tell me; is it wisdom to keep it anonymous?"

"I see your point," Liam meekly assented. "You have my silence."

"Thank you," she returned caustically, and turned to Steven. "As for the matter between you and me, human. From day one, you have challenged me. As you are now aware, I made the escape route. I also set this place up. If you intend to remain here, you will follow the rules. If you cannot, you are free to leave. My guidelines are for safety..."

"And just what does that have to do with what happened in there?" Steven challenged. "You were having a temper tantrum!"

At his side, Liam growled his disapproval. "Human, what am I going to do with you?"

"Well, she did say, I was supposed to take care of, and protect, Amara and TaTa..."

Liam shook his head in frustration.

****

Liam was aggravated at the human man; Amara was beside herself because Steven persisted in defending her and defying Susa, and that idiot human male was filled with such a mix of feelings, he couldn't sort them out. Susa sensed all this in one overpowering parcel, feeling besieged herself.

How does Liam handle it? Oh, yes. I forgot. He's only a mental; they forgot to give him the empathy gene!

Angrily, Susa turned from the roiling turmoil, and stamped back to the cabin.

The heck with them all!

But inside were the many others; minds with unspoken questions; musings of self indulgence and gratification, a mad house, a cesspool of human thought.

Susa gritted her teeth, and went for food.

When the others came in from the gardens, she had cloaked her mind, and schooled her features so most could not see her distress.

Chapter 28

Like a dorm mother, it was Downy's habit, so she could keep on top of things, to watch over what went on in the living room behind her. While she and Reva were doing up the dishes, she studied Susa, through the mirror at one side of the sink.

She's acting melancholy again...probably take off for the woods soon. If only she'd attach to the new Noor male...

Aw, but, he looks too much like Loki...

Downy sighed, and delved deeper into the soap suds.

****

As she stood drying dishes, Reva could see the alien woman, as well.

"What is Susa's story?" she asked quietly.

Downy sighed, and shook her head. "I'm afraid our Noor female is none too happy. I haven't seen her smile, since we came to the surface."

"So, she came down once before? To get you?"

"No. Actually, Susa spent time in the breeder pens..."

"Oh, you joke! That's not funny..." But, as Downy did not rescind her comment, Reva progress to what she thought was the obvious conclusion.

"Where is her baby?"

"They did not breed her..."

As the implications imagined fled through her mind, Reva felt a growing nausea.

"What happened?" she asked with apprehension.

"She nearly died in the cells...that's how she was made Noor."

"What do you mean?"

"She was once human, like you or me."

Disbelieving, Reva stared at the other woman. After a time, she decided it best not to know the details, but posed another question instead.

"So...why is she so sad...now, that she is free?"

Downy scrubbed forcefully at the pot in the water, finally, declared with a casual shrug.

"Someone broke her spirit..."

"Who?"

A long silence followed, and at last, Reva realized Downy was not going to disclose the rest. Either she didn't know, or she was keeping confidential.

****

Susa had had enough! She fled from the cabin, flying through the trees at a blur. When she was certain, she was beyond the psychic reach of the Noor male, she let the lethal feelings come to the fore.

Water. Help! Too many voices. Madness!

The many thoughts could be shut away, but it was the men, she found most unbearable.

That human! Always, filled with venom. When will he stop plaguing me?

And Liam! With his constant probing!

His gentle care and offered protection, reminded her of Loki. But, she didn't want to trust, nor forgive.

Not yet!

And that made the anger explode to the surface.

Trees in her way; banging against them, as if she were blind; ripping at them with her extended claws; tearing deep gouges from the tender bark.

Panting, she fell to her knees at the pond's edge. Her skin felt like fire, yet she shivered with cold. Angrily, she slashed at her own flesh, scarring the tissue in her wrath; deep cuts bleeding, sores oozing.

Then she was naked, plunging into the cold, shocking, depth of the placid pool, swimming with hard, powerful strokes to the distant, loud, plunging cascade; under the waterfall, where breath was taken in with difficulty, kick-starting the system, with its violent, constant battering.

Ten minutes later, Susa emerged from the water, healed. She willed her surroundings to repair the devastation done by her own hands, and the woods became serene, and pristine, once more. Then, she dropped against the bole of a nearby tree, and burst into sobs.

****

Feather had gone to the woods to get away from the crowd. A little open space always had a calming effect. It brought her near to the good spirit creatures.

It also eased the nausea.

A gust of wind seemed to brush by her, then was gone.

Breaking from the trees into a clearing by a waterfall, she heard the wrathful screaming. There was Susa at the water's edge.

Not wanting to be seen, and guessing that the Noor woman would want privacy, Feather stepped back, and hid behind the bushes.

The power of the being's abilities, and wrath, appalled her. By the time Susa disappeared into the water, Feather was visibly shaking. Yet still, she waited, unseen.

When Susa stepped from the water totally unscarred, and the damaged surroundings miraculously returned to unequaled beauty, the aboriginal wondered, if she was seeing a vision, or had imagined, what had gone on before.

The Raven plays tricks with my mind!

Susa sank to the foot of a tree, and began sobbing uncontrollably. It was then, Feather realized, the Noor was in desperate need of a friend.

No one would have faulted Feather if she had fled, for anyone else would have done so. But, instead, she rose up from her covering, and putting fear aside, ran to the other, without a second's thought.

"Oh, dear! You have a demon inside you," cried Feather. "You do good; it is best to cast it out..."

Susa moaned. "Oh, gosh! How much did you see?"

"I have watched others fighting their drug demons," Feather consoled.

In an effort to comfort, she attempted to gather the Noor against her bosom.

"Do not feel ashamed. I have witnessed much worse, and...have seen them win. Just let the good spirit take over."

"Oh, you don't understand!" Susa fought against the embrace. "We are...two!"

"Aren't we all," the native agreed. "One side is good; the other evil. Like the Raven, when it is trickster."

"Neither of us is evil!" Susa clarified. "One is the aggressor/warrior; the other is Healer/compassion."

With a fleeting movement, she batted at the tears, and mournfully continued.

"But as it stands, we are both so angry right now, frustrated, and...neither can get release. It drives us to madness! Without proper male balance, a dual female is self-destructive, a violent deranged creature. I do this to stabilize us..."

"Seems to me, it would be simpler to just give the guy a chance..."

Susa drew back from the human, staring at Feather with incredulity.

"Oh, you think I'm blind?" Feather chuckled. "I heard Liam ask you, back in the tunnel...I am a woman too. I can judge, when a man's gotten under your skin."

Susa hissed like an annoyed cat.

"A mental male is platonic; the mind balance! He is ruled by logic, not by flesh!"

Then she moved to sit alone, yet still remained close beside. The Noor woman was silent so long, thinking, Feather thought she meant to ignore her indefinitely.

Well, at least she's calm again.

"What are you doing out here, anyway?" Susa finally challenged. "No one comes this far in from the river. This is my private place..."

"Oh, the morning sickness rides my back," Feather joked. "Though it does seem to come all the time, and not just at meal times. It just takes the smell of cooking. Darn men, anyway, eh? I just needed fresh air...and space...like you."

Suddenly, a piece of toast appeared in the Noor's hand. She offered it to Feather.

"Eat," she ordered quietly. "Then we'll go back in."

Chapter 29

Late the next afternoon, Susa stepped across the threshold into the cabin. Downy met her, worry in every action. All around the two, people were already enjoying the evening meal. Liam was one of them. Steven and Amara also sat nearby, with little TaTa, feeding her.

"The baby is stuck," declared Downy anxiously. "I can't seem to turn it, and it's been way too long. I'm afraid, we will lose them both."

"I know," Susa agreed. "That's why I came in."

Liam was annoyed. "Why didn't you ask me for help?" he demanded indignantly, setting his plate aside, and standing up. "I am medic. I also know human anatomy."

"Don't need a male," Downy and Susa said, almost in unison.

"What is wrong with you females?" Liam declared hotly. "Do you prefer the woman...and child...to die?"

Susa turned to him, and for once her words were soft spoken. "I am Instant Healer, Liam," she reasoned quietly. "Are you?"

"No...but, I could assist."

"Come then...maybe..."

Amara sprang up. "Let me come, too, Susa...I could encourage, give comfort..."

"Yes, Amara...give the little one to Steven."

Like a convoy, a menagerie of characters followed Downy into a back room. Here a disheveled Filipino woman lay exhausted from days of labor. Reva who was mopping her forehead with a damp cloth, looked up with worry lines on her brow.

"Everyone keep back against the wall unless needed," Susa ordered curtly, moving to the bedside.

Liam and Amara followed her, while Steven moved out of the way to stand against the far wall.

****

Steven had never seen a woman give birth. During his sojourn in the dungeons of Bom's prison, when occupied, the delivery cubicle was the one place he'd been forbidden to enter. Also, having no offspring of his own, he'd not had the occasion on the surface, either.

When the pregnant woman began to pant, and then to scream, as if having a temper tantrum, Steven nearly messed himself.

Suddenly, he became more worried for TaTa, than his own discomfort. He pressed the face of the baby girl against him, covering with his arms, so she wouldn't hear or see.

As Liam moved back beside him, Steven got a full view of what was happening, and nearly passed out. Liam touched his shoulder, as if to reassure, and grinned broadly.

"You could have warned me," Steven said in a shaky voice. "I suppose, you've seen something like this before. I haven't!"

Liam's grin widened.

"Do you good to watch," he stated unfeelingly. "Witness the result of man's promiscuity."

Steven shivered.

****

Liam's attention was suddenly drawn to Susa. She had dropped to her knees to the side of the delivering woman.

"Susa, you have never healed to this extent before," he warned quietly. "My physical is Instant Healer, and I know of what I speak. To take on another's condition will be excruciating. If you need energy, please, will you ask for my support?"

She looked up at him, hesitated a moment, then nodded agreement.

****

At first Susa kept her mind only surface. Closing her eyes, she ran her hands along the sides of the woman's belly, and sensed deep within the womb.

The baby is crossways, the cord around the one arm and throat. If it were just around the infant's neck, we'd have a stillborn by now.

"Breathe deep," she quietly ordered of the stressed mother.

With her mind, forcing the child to move slowly, Susa watched as the tiny form rotated on a leisurely, revolving, forty-five degree turn, and as it did, the arm was pulled closer to the body, releasing the cord. Next, Susa mentally envisioned the cord slipping over the head. Now the baby was unencumbered, and in the right position.

The exhausted woman was going into another contraction, at the very brink of losing consciousness. Susa moved her hand up to catch the other's in her own. At the connection, she gasped with shock, as she became one with the deliverer's feelings.

A jarring flood of jumbled experiences hit her like a punch in the gut: moist fevered skin; wet thighs; nausea; a crash of hot, deep, penetrating ache across belly, and riding up the back.

I'd forgotten how agonizing labor can be.

The idea was barely a second's thought. Soon, she had to grit her teeth to keep from screaming out the agony for release. Susa doubled over...the real pregnant one passed out.

She willed the infant forward, down the canal. The head was crowning. Now it was out between the legs.

Susa sat back on her heels, releasing the hand, and the link, between herself and the patient. In her own consciousness again, she felt sudden, overwhelming weariness. But the birth was now nearly complete.

The body of the child moved with unexpected rapidity. It slipped greasily into her outstretched, waiting hands.

Suddenly, Liam knelt down beside her. Susa was panting with the overloaded effort.

"Take...baby," she gasped weakly. "I need...to rest...finish for me."

Liam quickly took her place.

****

With the skill of long practice, Liam took over. To the amazement of those around, his movements were gentle, swift, and careful for one of his size. He took the small brown infant, clamped the cord at both ends, severed it at the junction of the baby's navel, and cauterized. Turning the small one over, Liam ran his large hand across the boy's back. He coughed, then began to cry. Liam handed the child to Downy at his side.

"Keep him warm now..."

Covering the mother for privacy, Liam moved his hands down her still distended belly. The now conscious woman, gave a quiet sigh; there was a rush of liquid, and the sheets turned red with the coming of the after birth.

Downy had passed the new born to Amara. As if anticipating what was needed, she gathered up a basin with warm water and some cloths, and with Reva, she approached the bed.

"Clean them up," Liam ordered softly. "I will see to Susa."

Surprised, all eyes turned toward the Noor female, wondering why she needed care. Susa had crawled to a corner, sat, legs pulled up, arms hugging them, pale as a ghost, eyes closed, face pinched, as if in agony.

Liam knelt beside her; touched her hand.

"It's a shock to the system that first time," he observed quietly. "Want help?"

Without opening her eyes, Susa gave a barely discernable nod.

He moved beside her, gathered her to his lap, holding her spoon-like, tightly against him. After that, the two seemed oblivious of those around them, as Steven, with baby TaTa, was shooed from the room. The new mother was washed, sheets and covers replaced, and the clean, wrapped, now blissfully sleeping new born, placed beside his parent.

The room went silent, emptied. Soon mother slipped away into slumber, as well.

It seemed, so did the two Noor, their even breathing the only evidence they were still alive.

****

It was breakfast the next morning, before Liam and Susa came through the bed chamber door, closed it softly behind them, and put in an appearance in the dining room.

The atmosphere in the room went to one of tense expectation, and awe.

"I'm starving!" Susa declared, to break the ice.

At the feeble attempt at humor, Liam chuckled.

Downy moved in from the kitchen with a plate of pancakes.

Well, if we aren't to be given an explanation, the least I can do is feed this pair!

Chapter 30

"Noor male!"

The yell came from the edge of the trees just beyond the shore. It was rare, one of the women came to the river while the men were bathing. It was one of Susa's rules.

Liam searched for the source of the voice, and there in plain view, was the tiny native woman called Feather. She was bending over, her hands on her knees, trying to catch her breath, as if she had run all the way there.

He quickly wished his garments on his person, then strode across the sandbank toward her.

"Susa needs you," Feather gasped, barely able to get the words out.

Steven came up beside them, still buttoning his shirt.

"What's wrong?" he demanded, immediately assuming the worst.

"The dogs have found us," Feather revealed, with fear in her tone. "Susa sent me as soon as she sensed them, before they had even reached the compound. Told me to get the Noor male; she can't fight them off alone. There are too many."

"Crap!" exclaimed Steven. "And all the men are here, except for the sentries."

"Norris and another were on duty...they didn't warn us," Feather revealed. "I think the Roog must have killed them..."

"Steven!" Liam ordered, turning quickly to the man. "Bring her! Carry her!"

"But, that will slow me down!"

"Do you always have to argue?" Liam retorted in annoyance. "Can't you trust me by now? Do you want her to fall into their hands, be breeder stock, once again?"

"Sorry. Didn't think..."

But Liam had turned around, and took off in a blur.

****

Susa yelled to the two women in the kitchen. "Get the others to the garden!"

"Why?" asked Reva.

"Because, it's surrounded by the thorn hedge," Downy answered for her. "I'll go get the babies. Amara is nursing; mother and new born still sleeping..."

"Hurry, Downy!" Susa cried urgently. "We haven't much time. And I need to prepare my defense barrier, but...I'll have to be behind the hedge to do so, so they can't attack me while I'm in mental mode."

"Okay. You go," Downy agreed. "We'll get them all to safety, as quickly as we can."

****

Liam got there just as the last of the women were fleeing through the garden gate. Downy carried the new born boy, while Reva was helping the unsteady mother across the threshold of the opening.

He was yet at too far a distance to attack himself, when a huge Rottweiler Roog caught up to Downy, grabbed her by the neck, stopping her in midstride.

The beast raised the helpless woman above the ground, shook her violently. When that did not dislodge the burden she carried, his other paw grasped her by the legs, pulled and twisted. The result was, the snapping of her back, just below the shoulder blades.

The old woman went limp. The infant dropped from useless arms, plunging, like a slow motion missile, toward the ground.

Liam thought willed the baby to freeze suspended in midair, but the Noor was still out of range to effect a long term manipulation. It held only a second, then time seemed to speed up.

The tiny body hit the soil with such force, it spattered liquid pieces of blood and matter against the nearby trunks of trees, and the peat beneath.

Liam had no time to think of the tragedy that had just played out. He had suddenly realized, Amara and her baby girl were caught between the cabin and the Roog blocking the gate. The Roog had dropped his first victim, and was heading for the pair.

Liam had no choice but to engage in mortal combat. After all, he was warrior trained.

****

Steven ran as hard as he could, but even though Feather hardly weigh more than ninety-five pounds, and was no taller than five feet, the burden of the native woman was slowing him incredibly. The other men soon caught up; some even passed them.

He chaffed at the need to carry the girl, but Steven also knew, she would die by Roog hands if he left her on her own. He could now see the dogs were on a killing spree, taking no prisoners.

"Put me down," Feather pleaded. "I've got my second wind."

"No! Liam ordered me to take care of you. He'll break me in pieces, if something happens to you."

"Please," she begged. "We'll both get there quicker, if you let me run, too."

He finally gave in, set her on her feet, but took her hand. The cabin was close, just ahead.

****

As they rounded the trees into the yard, Steven never expected what they came upon. Liam was fighting for his life, going paw to claw with a giant Roog. The Noor/Feline had his talons extended, and they were formidable weapons.

Then Steven noticed, just behind the fighting duo, something that nearly stopped his heart. Amara and TaTa were trapped against the cabin.

Oh, God! Oh, God!

Feather and Steven stopped dead in their tracks. He dropped her hand.

Where is Susa? Man! Female! Where is your defense?

At the corner of his eye, Steven saw movement. A second Roog was beside them, almost upon him. He caught up a thick dead branch at his feet, and went to meet the beast.

But...suddenly, it was gone. Just vanished.

Did Susa do that?

****

Far away, on Dia's huge spaceship home, in the presently quiet med centre, Kimon was making notations on his small viewer screen, while Loki cleaned instruments nearby. The Noor suddenly straighten, and began growling ominously.

At the abrupt, unusual behavior from his normally gentle Instant Healer, Kimon started.

After a moment, he realized, his foster son was sensing something no one else could see.

"What is it?"

Again, Loki hissed viciously. Against the white of the sheet of the cot he worked by, his claws extended, and for a second appeared bloodied. Kimon stepped back, shivered, as insight and apprehension collided.

Then Kimon drew himself up, collecting his wits.

"Liam fights the Roog," Loki revealed, at last.

This time, it was his foster father's turn to answer with a growl.

Loki stiffened, then his face took on an expression of extreme distress.

"He...had to kill..." he declared sadly.

"Ha!" Kimon retorted with fervor. "Do not grieve for an enemy!"

Loki shook his head in disagreement. "Anytime life is ended is a tragedy," he returned quietly, adding: "When a Noor takes that life...it scars us."

Kimon grunted in derision.

"Is it finished?"

"No. I must have privacy, now. Liam needs my strength..."

"Okay. Go rest on the power bed."

Loki shambled off, leaving Kimon shaking his head, as he watched him go.

I will never understand their deadly connection. Each time I think I have it analyzed, it takes another form.

****

Liam turned from the body of the Roog, toward Amara.

"Get inside! Hurry!" He then spied Steven, Feather trembling at his side. "You, as well! Into the garden! Hurry! More are coming."

All around the human men were arriving, but their weapons were puny, mere sticks and stones...litterly.

"Everyone! Inside the garden thorn fence!" Liam yelled.

He was abruptly aware Susa was in his mind.

Get behind the barrier yourself! I can only send away one at a time! I need your power boost behind me!

So, Liam took his own words to heart, leading the group through the gate.

As he passed through it, he immediately felt the energy shield she was maintaining.

Just inside and to the side of the portal, Susa was on her knees, her eyes closed, in mental mode. Her physical person was totally exposed, unprotected. If a Roog had gotten through, or even one of the humans had touched her unexpectedly, he realized, she would have died at the contact.

Liam dropped to one knee beside her.

"Making physical contact," he warned, so she could brace herself. Then he caught both her hands in his.

Chapter 31

It was all over but to bury and mourn for the dead. With the combined power of a Noor mental male, and female, the two had sent every last Roog back to the dungeons from which they had come.

Liam was drained, barely able to stand, and Susa was not much better. They rose to their feet.

"If I had only realized the sentries were in trouble sooner; if I'd only been faster, I could have prevented the casualties, but I got distracted..."

"No blame should be placed..."

"But...it was all for nothing! The healing, the delivery...we lost the little one; instead of rejoicing, the mother will grieve now. Maybe, I should have left it be stillborn."

"No!" hissed Liam. "Never. What you did, at the time, was commendable. We cannot foresee future events. It is our function to help the living. The small one is with its Maker; we cannot save every soul."

As if she had not heard, Susa lamented. "Downy. And, Norris...my friends. They were so kind to me..."

She began to cry softly, and Liam finally realized, it was not just the shock of the loss, but extreme exhaustion rearing its ugly head.

"We need rest," he declared, gently leading her away toward the cabin.

"Not for long," she whispered. "They will soon mount another attack."

****

"We can't stay here!" Susa declared with force, as they sat eating alone at the kitchen table.

Liam agreed.

"I can take you off planet; that's what I came for. About a mile in the opposite direction from the river, I've had a ship cloaked, and hidden, all this time," Liam admitted. "If I had known you were so close, I would never have sought after Lana first..."

"As you so often have told me, nothing happens without a reason, and...you also say, the Almighty prepares our paths."

He chuckled at the apparent reversal of her mindset.

"Tell you what, male," Susa suggested. "I will go with you to your world, on one condition."

Liam studied her, raised an eyebrow.

"And that is?"

"All those on the compound go with us."

"It was my intent to take all. Never would I consider otherwise, but...the ship is equipped with only one hundred and twenty stasis pods, not enough for all the humans."

"We'll worry about that when we get there. Amara and her baby can always be doubled."

But Liam's mind was on another matter. He hesitated briefly, but finally, voiced the thought that was plaguing him.

"On my world, a female must chose a guardian...for safety."

"I accept you as mine," she agreed, without hesitation.

"You know what that means, do you not?"

"I agree. We will be considered as promised."

He let out a quick short breath, as if punched in the gut. She was suddenly so amendable, he had a hard time believing it was real.

"We do not have much time..." Susa said suddenly.

He opened his mind to distant vision, to see what she saw by seer sense.

"Bom has sent the Roog to the surface again."

She nodded.

"I can only jump with a few at a time..."

"Not that way; not enough time. We will again have to make a trek through the woods."

"Then we'd better get moving..."

****

Thor settled the shuttle to the ground, as a huge bay door opened in mid air, exposing the inner workings of the cloaked ship.

"There it is," Uel informed him. "Let's get inside before we are seen."

They had no sooner settled; Thor was studying the images on the viewing panel of the larger ship, when he spied the humans outside, running through the trees.

He immediately surmised what was happening; hit the door image on the board, to hoist the large outer panel. Without hesitation, the menagerie of humankind made for the opening.

Then, he caught sight of Liam. He was carrying a small dark haired Filipino woman.

****

After setting his burden down, the Noor did not seem surprised, that Thor and Uel were there.

"You came by shuttle? How big is it?"

"A twenty..."

"And how many stasis pods?"

"Twenty-two."

"Excellent!" Liam nodded toward those milling around in the bay. "I want all humans placed in stasis, immediately. Explain, that there is nothing to fear; it is for their comfort and safety during the journey. When you have finished, you and Uel enter one, as well."

Thor frowned. "You do not want me to man the controls?"

"We will be traveling the quick way."

"With so many aboard?" Thor exclaimed astounded.

Liam grinned. "I have a secret power source..."

Thor knew better then to question. Liam was the strategist, and was always truthful.

"Oh, before you go, I have something to tell both of you," Liam added. "Thor; the eldest member in Reva. She has recently suffered the loss of a friend, and needs your special care. She is also your compatible..."

Thor raised a questioning eyebrow, but said nothing.

"And Uel; one is also compatible to you. The tiny one, called Feather. Her greatest wish is to be a healer. It will be up to you, how you win her."

Uel growled deep in his throat, with pleasurable anticipation.

****

Everyone was locked away in the deep sleep of stasis. Liam had just raised the ship to the upper atmosphere of Earth. He turned to Susa, seated beside him.

"Now, for the ultimate test of our combined abilities."

She reached for his hand without hesitation, knowing exactly what was needed. Instantly, the ship, and passengers had jumped into the region of space, just next to Dia's med ship.

Chapter 32

As soon as their craft gained entrance to the larger ship, Liam, himself, felt the shock of the mental barrage that hit Susa. He was already that connected to her feelings.

When she reached up, and touched the band that circled her forehead, he suddenly realized its function. Until now, he had thought it only an ornament, a jewelry, such as other females wore.

What a marvelous idea! A cushion to shut out the extra thought voices.

At her nervousness, he moved his arm to her shoulders, to reassure her.

****

As the huge door of the ship raised to expose them to a new world, terror ran rampant in the mind of Susa. It was like stepping back into her past, with all its uncertainties, animosities, and struggles. Never mind, she was now a powerful entity, inside she was still that old Althea, and that insecure individual, was extremely wary of facing her family.

Yes, she was aware. No one had to tell her. At the first encounter with Liam's mind, she had seen how her children had been integrated into Dia's nest. The details were sketchy, for the Noor male had not invaded the memories of her offspring, but Susa knew, they were all here; even her granddaughters, were on the ship.

The hardest part will be facing them.

Though, to all outward appearances, she appeared in control, inside, the mother of Nyle and Moriah, was quaking in her skin. All she could remember, about their past relationships, was controversy, neglect, and cruel rejection.

Sensing vaguely her hesitation, yet unable to explain the reasoning, Liam took her hand, to draw her across the threshold.

"No need to fear," he reassured. "My family will find you most endearing."

"Right!" she returned sarcastically. "As Steven often does."

He chuckled.

She sighed resolutely, and went with him.

"This is your world, Liam," she warned. "Until I am more familiar with it, I'll follow your leadership."

He nodded in agreement.

****

And there was Nyle, waiting to greet them. She almost did a double take.

He still looked every bit human: the reddish-blond hair, and green eyes, but the bearing had changed. Nyle now appeared more confident; he stood straighter, and moved with the lithe lightness of a cat on the prowl.

He has changed, both outwardly, and...in his mind.

And though, for a minute, the fear was overwhelming, Susa plunged into her son's thoughts to see, and...he did nothing to block her.

She read all that had taken place during the prior year, and was both shocked and pleased. Gone was his abusive nature, the cruel petulant humor, and self-indulgent lack of care for others.

He's grown up! But, can I trust that he'll stay that way?

Nyle chuckled, then sobered.

"Momma...I've been a brute to you in the past. I've learned a better way. I hope, I can make you proud of me in the future. Please, forgive me."

Susa shook her head, as if to clear it. In the past, Nyle never apologized, leave alone, ask forgiveness. It had always been: he was right; you were wrong.

This can't be my son. What did they do to him?

Behind her, Liam smiled knowingly.

Nyle laughed. He didn't need to be told he was pardoned.

A mother always forgives!

He hugged her exuberantly.

When he stepped back, Nyle was a picture of stoic control, and respectful seriousness. He looked to Liam.

"May I escort you and my mother?"

Liam nodded ever so slightly in approval. Then Nyle stepped to the other side of the one who had borne him.

****

Thor led the humans through the corridors at a rapid pace. Liam had ordered him to go the quickest and shortest route, and so, they were passing through the most dangerous part of the ship; the sleep quarters of the single warriors.

Without speaking to her, he had moved Reva to his side to walk with him, but she was unable to keep up with his constant strong stride, and at last, from mere frustration, for safety, he scooped her up into his arms. She gave a short squeal of fright when he did it, but quickly settled down.

He could sense the fear of the women following, and the pregnant ones, especially, were lagging dreadfully. All around, the warriors were leaving the comfort of their chambers to watch, each keeping pace in obvious anticipation.

"Females," whispered one excitedly.

Another answered. "Human...and they are heavy with young."

A third, declared optimistically: "Even though they are human, I hope one is compatible to me. I would treasure both her, and the young one."

But the males wore no translators. Thor knew, mercifully, the women could not understand the sibilant verbs of the Feline tongue. To them, the beasts around them were threatening.

He hissed at the warriors.

"Stop frightening them! You are not dogs! They think you want to eat their young."

"We help?" questioned the first who had spoken.

"Yes. Carry the females."

****

All around them, the shadows slunk; cats of every kind: some with long grey hair; others with white, fluffy fur. One had a doll-like face, eyes of blue; another was chocolate with sleek short hair and yellow eyes. There was one of tan almost honey colored coat, and this one, too, had yellow eyes.

But most disconcerting of all; every one of them, was at least over six feet tall.

When they scooped up their charges, some screamed, others swooned, and many fought feebly.

But the warriors were stronger than they, and in fact...gentle.

****

In the middle, walking between Nyle and Liam, even Susa was frightened. She moved over, until she was near touching the side of her promised one.

"Want me to carry you?" Liam asked quietly.

But, Susa bravely shook her head, and increased her pace, beside him.

****

Back at the very end of the line, Uel struggled to keep up, not because he was the smallest Feline male, but due to the fact, that his charge was simply too petite and delicate; she couldn't seem to keep pace anymore.

Uel was on constant alert, the fur of his back, standing on end, in apprehension. He chaffed at the gap that was widening by the minute, making them vulnerable to any predatory warriors, that might leave their quarters, and find the pair alone.

No matter that here on Dia's ship, the single guardians were of a more generous persuasion then elsewhere; he knew, even if this female was his compatible, any male had the right to challenge, and to seek to win her from him. It was the unspoken rule.

His thoughts went to the prison setting, where he had been raised, mostly by the inmates; Bom's prison establishment, where one had to fight for everything. Uel knew what was done to human female captives underground; he had served most of his term in the med bay there.

This poor little creature at his side, seemed not to have fared too badly, yet he knew scars could be hidden, festering beneath the surface, not visible to those on the outside. At this moment, his little Feather was struggling for breath, panting as if the air was no longer fresh; and he could endure that no more.

She was about four inches shorter than he, so he finally reached over, and lifted her into his arms. Then he sped up, to catch up to those far ahead.

Feather was light, like her name implied, and Uel was well muscled, strong beneath his long fur coat. He had not lost his sturdy physique, for here on the med ship, the Noor had a running track, attached to the home nest, and he joined many others in the attempt to keep up to Loki. Of course, no one ever caught Loki.

The smooth skin, of the woman in his arms, felt like silk, distracting him.

Oh, yes, Uel! You have a keeper here! I never imagined, I could be so lucky.

Chapter 33

"Get these creatures into diagnostics!" thundered Kimon irritably. "I want them out of my bay as soon as possible. Don't like humans..." he grumbled quietly to himself.

Thor hit the button on his throat translator device, shut it off, and switched directly to the Feline tongue.

"This one is mine!" he declared, gesturing to Reva at his side. "I take her for mate."

"Say, what?"

"It is my right! You heard me!"

Kimon hissed disapproval.

"This late in life? Are you mad?"

"Yes! And, not sure." Thor grinned broadly.

Kimon growled deep in his chest.

"Well, then...get her into a healing pod. Her age and physical deterioration has progressed to such a point, regular healing practices will not be enough. Her body clock needs regressing. Have a mechanical orderly help you program..."

As an afterthought, Kimon added: "While in there, sleep teach her, educate her in our rules and ways, and teach her our speech."

"I speak passable human..."

"I don't want human spoken in my nest!" Kimon declared venomously. "Do you hear?"

Thor growled ominously. "Remember, Kimon, I am the elder male here," he warned. "If I wish to speak to her in human, for privacy, it is my choice...but, I will educate her in our tongue."

"Spit!" The physician turned away conceding.

But Liam was nearby, and chose also to challenge his foster, speaking in the Feline tongue, so the humans only heard Kimon's one sided conversation, for the head physician never removed, nor shut down, his throat translator while on the floor. A Noor did not need the translator device; and could switch from tongue to tongue; they were all linguists.

"Uel also takes a human for mate."

Again Kimon hissed disapproval. "What is this, a conspiracy?" He growled, in evident disagreement with the circumstances. "Well, put her in a pod, as well, then. She no doubt has been damaged. And...she better not be a problem to Dia!"

"No, healing pod for Feather," Liam objected quietly. "She carries..."

Uel's head came up in shock.

Kimon spat in anger. "What are you two bringing into my nest?" And then, as another thought struck him, he turned on Uel. "You've already been intimate?"

"I did not know," Uel whispered.

"Then...perhaps you will leave this one?" Kimon said hopefully.

Uel raised to his full height, which brought him near to eyelevel with his superior, for Kimon was only five foot six. "No! Sir!" he returned with indignation. "My feelings stand!"

Liam, behind him grinned. Kimon spit with livid wrath.

"I send you two on a rescue, and you come back with a ship load of pregnant human females, and...males, of all things! You'd better have a good explanation, and...I...will, hear it all when we are done here!"

Liam shook his head. "Go," he said in human, to the unfortunate pair. "I'll mollify his mood."

Kimon growled. "Liam! Stop using that disgusting human gibberish. I know you are trying to keep me from understanding!" He thundered: "Get out of here! You! All! Teach them Feline! The human languages are forbidden in our nest!"

****

"And register all the other human females in the compatible data bank," Kimon bellowed. "Shoo! All humans!"

Steven didn't know what such a bank was for, but suspicion drove him to action. He quickly realized, this meant separation from Amara and TaTa, and he couldn't have that. So, gaining encouragement at the other's successful encounters, he bravely took on Kimon, himself.

"That one it mine!" he shouted quickly, pointing to the young woman with her infant.

Kimon turned, hissed. "What is that stupid male so worked up about?"

Liam stepped in, slipping a translator around the human's throat, so Steven could fight his own battle.

"She's mine!" Steven repeated, almost panicking.

Kimon grunted. "This she is your mate?"

"Ah, if she'll have me?" To Amara, he added: "If you never let me touch you, I'll understand. I'll honor that..."

The translator told it in English, but when Amara answered, without the device, she could not speak in Feline. And Kimon understood neither exchange.

"I belong to him," Amara agreed.

Kimon growled. "Enough of this! What do you want done with them?" he asked of Liam.

"Put them in our home nest?" Liam asked, obviously feeling he skated on thin ice. "He has bravely been my protector, more than once."

Kimon spat viciously. "Humans everywhere! Our nest will be full of them!"

"Oh, Poppa," chided Liam. "Put aside your prejudices for a change..."

"Humans are an abomination. They cannot be trusted! I'll not have this! I'll not sit by, and..."

"I know you have been brutalized by a human, Poppa, but...it's time to let it go."

But Kimon remained adamant, and would hear none of it.

Through the many exchanges, Susa had been silently observant. Now, she stepped forward, gave one simple statement to change Kimon's mind.

"If I were to take revenge for what has been done to me, Kimon, the whole Universe would pay..."

Kimon turned, and as he looked into the now, rainbow hued mirrors of the Noor female, his jaw dropped.

"You..." he gasped. "What do you see?"

"I see much. And from this moment, the past is pacified."

Kimon started, gasped, and doubled over, as if in sudden pain. His eyes went wild with awe. When he came up to stand erect again, his breath, and his words, came with soft spoken disbelief.

"What have you done to me?" he whispered.

"You are whole again, male," Susa declared quietly. "When next you lie with your mate, give her the kit, she has longed for, for so long."

Kimon let out a soft breath. "I was castrated..."

"By a human. Yes. I know. It has been undone. Now, be angry no more."

Tears formed in the old physician's eyes. "What are you?" he whispered.

"Doesn't matter," Susa said, switching the conversation back to the original controversy. "What of the humans? Will you allow them in your nest?"

Kimon shook his head, as if to clear it.

"Huh," he said. "Yes! They are welcome in my nest."

Chapter 34

"Oh, momma! Look at you," exclaimed Moriah with awe, as she approached the bedside. "So beautiful, and...looking so young."

Susa opened her eyes. She was reclining on a exam bed, in a far corner of the med bay, after enduring the thorough assessment, Kimon had insisted upon. Still attached to her left temple, was the compulsory education disk, though she had long ago absorbed its extensive programming.

Before the two women could interact, Liam appeared beside Susa. He reached out to remove the teaching implement.

Totally ignoring her daughter, Susa spoke to him in a mere whisper.

"I want all the Noor knowledge available."

Liam nodded in understanding, and disappeared to get it.

Not to be deterred, Moriah moved up to the bedside.

"Momma...forgive me. Please. I am sorry. For all the times I failed to consider your needs; for being cruel, and unloving toward you in the past..."

Immediately, Susa intruded into the younger woman's thoughts, to see how genuine she was. As their minds connected, and Susa read all the recollections of her daughter's past year, she was appalled at the violent battle, that had ensued, as a result of her being kidnapped. It put a whole new light on Moriah's mating, and for a moment, Susa's protective mother nature, grew angry at Shiveron.

Then the memories went to the male's sacrifice, the suffering Moriah had endured, the healing of her obstinate daughter, and at last, culminated in the gentleness of her lover. Shiveron was exonerated.

Susa realized, as had always been the case from childhood, her daughter had learned most lessons the hard way.

Surely, my daughter cannot have changed so profoundly?

"Oh, I hope so, momma," Moriah exclaimed earnestly, reading her mother's skeptical thought. "I never knew I was such a vicious lost soul..."

And quite unexpectedly, the two were embracing. The elder could not but give mercy. Forgiveness, came easy then; mother love rose abundantly.

****

It was when they parted, Susa noted Iora. As so often in recollection, her multi-racial granddaughter was standing, like a silent shadow, behind her mother.

Memories flooded over Susa:

All the times, she'd been ignored by her granddaughter, as if she were unimportant; refused the courtesy of her help, and been belittled by Iora, as she declared, she was the superior, ultimate authority on any subject. It was as if, no time at all had passed.

The elder expected the same engrained behavior, and so, when the dark eyed, raven haired beauty, with the clear, caramel complexion, stepped timidly forward, Susa was extremely surprised at the attitude of remorse and repentance.

"Grandma..."

Iora was trembling with pent up apprehension. "Please...I'm...sorry, too." She took a quick breath to gain courage. "I have learned the error of my attitudes. I hope...that in the future, I will love, serve, and respect you, as the Leader you are meant to be."

Is this Iora? I never thought I'd see the day.

"Please, forgive, grandma...for my past self-indulgence. I accept your right to scruff me...if ever I fall back into my old habits."

Susa laughed outright. "Either you have really grown up, or...they have switched my granddaughter."

Iora dropped her eyes, embarrassed.

"No, grandma; it's really me," she finally said, at a near whisper. "I owe it all to Dia..."

"Well, then," Susa declared with candor. "I believe this Dia must be a better mother than I ever was!"

"Oh, no, momma!" Moriah vehemently objected. "It was I who refused to listen to your wise counsel, and I passed that negative viewpoint on to my daughter..."

"Don't excuse her entirely," Susa admonished.

"Yes, mom," cut in Iora. "I had plenty of prejudices of my own."

Susa chuckled. It was refreshing to listen to them, even if they still had a perchance to argue with each other.

At least, it is a respectful debate, now.

Moriah brought her back from her contemplations.

"The fact is, momma," she stated. "Dia is much stronger, and...better at threatening, and enacting, discipline."

Susa grinned. "I guess, she would need to be, to handle those as large as Liam."

And, as if he'd been summoned by the mention of his name, Liam appeared at their side, the new information disk in his hand.

****

While Liam was attaching the teaching device, Moriah and Iora slipped away. Susa failed to note this, as she was abruptly inundated with copious amounts of new knowledge.

Almost instantly, Susa had absorbed all the small recorder had contained.

Liam chuckled. "I should have expected that," he chided himself. "One such as you, eats facts like candy. Do you realize, even I, have been unable to process some of what is on that disk?"

"That's because it wasn't meant for you. The Essence prepared it as a record to refresh her memory, should she lose some of her faculties, as the result of torture."

Liam's jaw dropped. "Really?" he said amazed. Then removed the disk from her forehead. "Then, it has been given to the right individual...it will help you rule."

She let that one go, without comment.

Liam turned to leave.

Suddenly, Susa was flooded with an overwhelming loneliness, and a heavy homesick dread. Inside her, Tilk whimpered, as old memories surfaced, flashing through the Essence's mind. Susa immediately realized the pleasant remembrances, and horrid encounters, were not her own.

She shivered.

"Wait...Liam," Susa called hesitantly.

Already steps away, he turned back.

"Please?" she pleaded softly. "Will you..."

"Comfort-cuddle?" He grinned, returned, and gently moved up on the bed beside her.

She could feel his heart racing excitedly, as he slipped his arms around, and settled in behind her. It was then, the Noor female realized, this was the first time she had actually asked, and accepted his care, without the need being crucial. She had stepped across a threshold.

Susa relaxed against him, and Liam settled down.

It did not take long for the pair to move into deep slumber, for the stresses of societal reintegration had been taxing to both of them.

Chapter 35

Reva hadn't felt this good in years. It was like being twenty-one again, not simply because her body clock had slowed, returning her to the health, and youthfulness of that age, but she was experiencing a giddy anticipation, she could not explain. The prospects: of seeing the peoples of many worlds; encountering previously unknown tastes and smells; touching and seeing beauty unlike that found on Earth, was a heady inspiration, but it did not account for the expectation that seemed to spread from her belly, all the way to her breast.

To be young again! Does that mean to love again?

Her breath came with difficulty, as approval mirrored in the eyes of the large Feline male, who had accompanied her to the healing pod, and now helped her step out of it.

She was naked, for clothes had been a hindrance within the unit, and though the male had turned his back, as she disrobed to get in, she had been much embarrassed by her flabby and wrinkled person.

Now, she was aware of curves that had returned, self-conscious once again, as he handed her garments, and once more, turned his back to give her privacy. Until she was fully attired, he did not speak, or turn toward her.

From the teaching disk, she knew Feline custom. For a male to attend her meant, he had either been appointed her guardian, or...he had chosen to seek her as a mate. She also realized, it was up to her to respond, if he asked.

He no longer wore the translator at his throat; obviously he was meaning for this to be a moment of confidentiality. When he spoke, she understood perfectly his Feline speech.

"I am Thor. I declare, I will be your protector. All I ask in return, is that you will be my companion."

"Companion? As in mate?"

He grinned boyishly, then sobered.

"I will serve you; only touch you if you wish."

Reva shivered. Warmth spread across her cheeks; even her ears began to burn.

He is asking to my...husband. Oh, so romantic!

"I...I haven't...ah, done such things in many years."

"Needs will differ now," he boldly declared. "Your body has been rejuvenated."

His eyes travelled appreciatively over her form.

"I'll say!" she agreed.

Thor chuckled.

"Do we have an agreement?" he asked.

At her slight hesitation, he added: "However, if you wish, you may chose another."

The disappointment in his voice was not lost on Reva. Teasingly, she returned: "No. I'll take a chance on you."

Thor grinned good-naturedly.

"Do you wish for me to follow you, or to lead?"

"You go first. You know the way to where we are headed next."

"Shall we, then?"

He moved forward, down a side passageway, with Reva close behind. They took the private elevator direct to Dia's nest.

****

Susa was immediately shy and reserved, as she entered the home nest of Liam. But she need not have worried about her reception; Twila was upon her almost instantly, bubbling with welcome. The most disconcerting fact was, Liam simply vanished from the suite, leaving Susa in the hands of the females.

"Time to take a bath!" Twila declared, taking her by the hand, as if Susa were a mere girlish companion, not the elder of the two.

The wall panel slid open, to reveal the blue marble tiles of an immense indoor swimming pool. Waves of girlish laughter flooded out toward them.

"We'll do the works!" Twila enthused. "Have you ever had a manicure or a pedicure?"

Susa cringed, drew back from the door, as the unbidden memory surfaced violently.

Bom. "Pretty red toes."

She sucked in her breath. Susa hadn't expected to revert to the horror of the past.

"Oh! No!" Twila cried, reading the unguarded remembrance. "We must erase that one! Replace it with something better."

The door panels slid closed behind them, and Susa stood trembling. She had also forgotten, she was in a houseful of telepaths. Her mental guard went up, immediately.

To steady her equilibrium, Susa gazed about her.

The air smelled of spiced incense, cinnamon, and apple blossoms. There was a mist rising from the warm water, and the sound of the gentle, peaceful rush of the waterfall, cascading from the far wall, brought back memories of the private Earth grotto, to which she had so often fled.

"That's better," encouraged Twila, sensing the change of mood. "Now, we have girl time. In here, no one is the older, none are too young, even the humans..."

Twila wave a hand to encompass those scattered about.

At the water's edge, lounging on towels, were those Susa already knew: Moriah, Iora, Feather and Reva, even Amara with baby TaTa. One present, she hadn't seen since infancy.

Kaudy. The granddaughter I've been denied the chance to get to know...until now.

"Even the humans," Twila finished. "Are now family...on equal footing. We enjoy...be like young again."

Susa laughed.

My daughter-in-law is a treasure!

From there, they went to slathering skin in perfumed soap; shampooing silken tresses, swimming out to the falls to wash it all off. Then it was toweling off, painting toes and fingernails in brilliant colors, lubricating bodies with scented oils, massage, and finally, dozing, pleasantly relaxed.

When the call came for dinner, there were no longer inhibitions...at least not among the females.

****

"Where is Loki?" asked Shiveron, as the two couples sat in the corner, eating their evening meal.

Liam shrugged. "Avoiding...said he wasn't hungry. As per usual, since his return from the prison, he evades any intimate encounter with me. But...I'll give him a little more time, before I deal with it, as I now am more familiar with what went on in the prison."

Shiveron regarded his foster brother questioningly, but Liam had shut away the knowledge of what he had learned, and was unreadable.

The younger male gathered the empty plates, rose and took them to the kitchen. This night, the males were responsible for clean up, as Dia had done the cooking.

****

"Liam!" Dia's tone brooked no argument. "I will see your new promised in my private chambers." She paused a second, before adding: "Alone!"

"Yes, momma."

Liam quietly, gently encouraged Susa toward Dia's home ante.

"Do not fear her," he admonished. "Her snarl is worse than her bite. Look for her gentle side."

Then he left the two alone together.

Chapter 36

Dia turned with feigned anger.

"Who are you, she? What are you?"

And the Introvert female was ready, prepared with a most unanticipated answer.

"Know you not, Dia?" asked Tilk. "Do you not recognize me, friend?"

Dia gasped, as the pleasant blue human eyes turned to the ever changing hues of many colors. The insistent voice continued:

"From the day we first met as children, and played together in the fields, we were like sisters."

Shakily, Dia completed the picture. "You never treated me as other humanoids did, as if I were, but an animal..."

"You remember..." Tilk returned fondly.

"Oh, but how is this possible?" Dia pleaded. "They said you were dead."

"Remember, a long time ago, I told you...the Roog may kill the body, but never the mental. They tormented my physical until she could exist no longer, but the Essence...they put me in a stasis box; thought they could hold me..."

"Oh, Tilk," Dia whispered in awe. "And...now?"

"I found a suitable Soul Saver, a gentle creature worthy to be junctioned to me. She was so battered, and still is...treat us gentle."

Dia sighed, and for long moments stood in wonder, trying to fathom what had been revealed.

"What do I call you? I feel I should bow at your feet...you are..."

"Speak not of that, for now; it must remain hidden that the Universal Monarch survived. It will be our little secret...as in days of old, when I pretended to be a commoner."

They chuckled at the remembrance.

"Liam does suspect, but he does not fathom our full potential," Tilk informed. "Most Noor will shortly comprehend..."

"May I tell Kimon?"

"He already knows there is more to me than meets the eye. But...I forgot to answer your first question. We are now Tilk/Susa; however, my physical still needs much care to adjust. I believe you are the perfect one to help us with that. Give no special honor in public..."

"But you rule a species...you should show yourself to the Universe!" objected Dia.

"We are not yet ready. For what you have done all these years, protecting my people; when the time is right, you will watch with privilege, and honor, from the sidelines, as we take our place."

"My Lady..."

"I give my physical over to you now..."

****

As her eyes turned back to the normal blue, Susa sank to her knees, wailing.

"Help me, Dia!" she moaned fearfully. "I feel like I am demon invaded. Part of me wants this alien thing gone, the other part demands I keep her, because I know that without her I will die."

Tears of panic poured down the pale cheeks. "I am only an insignificant human, of little value, except...within my own family circle...I am no ruler!"

"But, that is the best kind of sovereign!" Dia affirmed reassuringly. "Such a one will be aware of the needs of the lesser beings."

"Oh, momma Dia," pleaded Susa. "I quake in my skin with fear; my other side is the mighty warrior, not me!"

"Ah, ah. My poor, poor dear," Dia murmured sympathetically. "Come, little one; Dia will mother you...and protect you!" she added with momentary venom.

The warning from Tilk, came only to her own mind.

Leave us fight our own battles, Dia. Only watch and comfort.

And Dia took to heart the inaudible caution, squelching her protective mother instinct, for the time being, but ever thereafter, she was extremely protective of this Noor female, even to defending her against her present favorite, Loki.

"We cuddle now," she proclaimed. "And I will ease your dilemma."

****

Like a small child needing reassurance, Susa dried her tears, and crawled into the lap of the elder Feline.

When the foster mother of Liam, wrapped her furry arms around the Noor female, to any other eye, it might have appeared, the reverse of the animal/human experience, so prevalent upon the planet she had just left. Though Susa was the larger, Dia seemed the possessor; the other, similar to the pet.

And so they sat conversing.

Susa told Dia how it had all begun; how Loki had disobeyed Bom, hiding her, as she was dying. How the physical of the junction pair had given of his life blood, and nearly forfeited his own life in so doing, all so she might keep hers.

However, she did not tell all: how far intimacy had gone, her feelings of rejection and abandonment, the anger toward Loki. But the wise, older Feline suspected much, and the rest, she did not need to be told.

Dia kept her counsel, not judging for or against the male, merely marveling how it had come about; concentrating instead, on the terror in the heart of the one in her arms.

Then knowledgeable Dia went to the crux of the matter; began giving a lesson on the wonderful workings of the Introvert Noor being that Tilk/Susa had become.

"Do not fear Tilk," she admonished. "She is your protector. Without you, she cannot be. Surrender when she is needed, for she is your knowledge, your power, and your reason."

"But I still have my own of all of these...except maybe, the power. On Earth we were taught such possession was evil."

"Huh!" grunted Dia. "And so once were we. But long ago, Tilk, and her other one, taught me differently."

For a moment, Dia seemed to drift into memory, then, she shook herself, and went on. "Yes, Tilk is deadly, a destroyer, but you...with your gentle goodness, can control her wrath."

"But how? When sometimes, I am so angry at the world, myself?"

"Ah, yes," Dia proclaimed. "Therein lies the problem. You try to fight her battle, when she is meant to fight yours."

"What then; I should just let her take over?"

"Yes, and no. Do not try to hold her at bay. Use her; work with her; guide her..."

"Me? Guide her? And just how do I do that?"

"By giving your gentle, kindhearted input...be your loving self. You will be much more at balance."

"Right now, I have a hard time doing that."

"You were chosen, because she felt, you could accomplish this."

Susa sat there thinking, trying to reason it out. Finally, she posed another question.

"How do you know all this, Dia? Explain about the other, your friend."

"Umm," Dia murmured. "The Noor Queen! The Essence is passed down from generation to generation. She holds the Noor race together. If this Noor spirit could be destroyed, the species would be no more. That is what the Roog misunderstand. They wanted only to stop the benevolent beings from policing them; the Noor were in their way. They did not realize, they had the key to their destruction...if, that is, it were possible to destroy her."

She paused, thinking through how best to present it. Deciding at last; she began at the beginning.

"The first pair was born on a humanoid world, one inside the other. When their powers first became evident, others feared her, confined her in an insane asylum. She lived long past the life spans of her jailors, and finally escaped.

"Then later, was born her junction partner; a male that could separate into two visible entities. When the two, and two, finally came together, they found the potential of their capabilities. They realized, they could use such power either for good or evil.

"Considering their personal maltreatment, the very fact they chose to be benevolent, speaks overwhelmingly in favor of the Noor nature. Since that time, the species has mostly been of human and Noor combination. Only recently, has Feline been added to the mix."

"And...how does she transfer, and why?" Susa asked.

"The how, I do not know," Dia admitted. "The why, is usually when the fleshly part of the being is unable to survive. Before that death, the Essence generally has searched out, and chosen, a worthy beneficiary, into which she moves her spirit essence just before passing. But in this instance, there was no time to prepare beforehand. If not for Loki's deed, Noor life would have eventually ceased to exist."

Susa hissed at the mention of the male physical. Her thoughts were suddenly on his misdeeds, not the good he had done.

"Loki betrayed us!" she growled with venom. "I should kill that male!"

Dia laughed, knowing full well it was Tilk who spoke, yet Susa seemed equally distraught.

"Many times, I have the same thought about my male. Kimon is a testy creature, but I have found, most of the time, rather than control him, it is more beneficial to give him his own way. It accomplishes more, to produce security and peaceful relationship, than any other method. As a result, love comes easier to him...I always reap the benefits in the end."

"I want Loki to...be repentant," Susa resolved. "I need that..."

"Ah. Vengeance. It never works well, little she," rebuked Dia. "Lack of forgiveness eats at the soul of the creature holding the grudge. I have seen it in my Kimon; I know of what I speak."

Susa began to cry softly.

"I know, hurt is hard to swallow," Dia encouraged. "It takes time to let go, but in the end, it is well worth it. Would you like me to intervene?"

"No," Susa resolved, wiping angrily at the betraying moisture. "I must try on my own."

But, Tilk had the last word in the end.

"Maybe, though, it wouldn't hurt to let him squirm a bit, first!"

Dia chuckled.

****

It was finally sleep time; all were settling down to rest. Liam had just curled up comfortably behind Susa. The others around them grew quiet; many still awake, but slowly lapsing into lazy somnolence.

The outer door slid open, and the last missing family member slunk in. Out of the pregnant stillness, Dia's voice hissed disapproval.

"Where have you been?"

"Last minute clean up, momma," a hesitant voice returned.

Susa went rigid.

"We missed you at the meal..." The reproof turned to a mother's consideration. "I've kept your meal warm for you."

"Not hungry, momma."

Dia hissed in annoyance. "Go to bed then!" And she turned into to Kimon, facing him.

The giant male looked about, spied his mental, and quietly eased over the mat toward Liam and Susa. He never got close enough to lie down.

Tilk hissed maliciously. Liam gasped in surprise; Loki stopped startled, then slowly slunk away, defeat in every movement.

A heavy silence of shocked surprise emanated from those around the three. After a time, each one settled down again.

That night, and many of the subsequent rest periods thereafter, Loki slept alone, in a far corner of the communal sleep mat.

Chapter 37

Steven liked the work assigned to him. Every day, at the entrance door leading into the Med Center, he stood guard, paired with either a Bear being, or one of the invisible Slither. He preferred it best, when it was one of the snake-like half humans, for then he felt as if, all were dependent upon his protection alone. Self-worth wasn't a flaw that had been erased by his programming.

The human had been trained in the methods of Warrior defense, given a laser wand weapon, and a thick metal rod, so that he could handle those larger than he that got out of hand. But the first strategy was always to be peaceable. Steven now belonged to the core group of the Noor nest, and it was his responsibility to exhibit the nonviolent nature of that healer clan.

After what Steven had seen of Liam's lethal, killer Feline claws, he had no wish to tangle with the males of the species, unless absolutely necessary.

The man had a full view of everything that took place on the vast floor. He could watch each patient, their care, and the methods used to heal each. He learned much, even though he was, but a warrior man.

Steven felt extremely content. In the home nest, he was allowed to care for Amara and TaTa; while at work, his charges were watched over by those around them. Every male of the nest took seriously the protection of the females from the clan; whether of Noor, Feline, Slither, Bear or Human; they were all family.

Amara and Reva had been incorporated as kitchen staff. With mechanical helpers, they prepared the meals for those on break, or small snacks for the injured or sick, under care in the med facility.

Dia, who had taken an instant liking to the human baby, supervised all that went on. While Dia worked in her office, most often as not, TaTa could be found playing nearby, or cuddling in the elder Feline's arms. Therefore, the little infant was no trouble at all. Though sometimes, she would pose the question: "Susa?", she was content to be told: "Busy."

Steven felt, life could only get better.

****

Even from the first, without being told, Feather had realized the fact, she'd been given to Uel. Now that she'd been educated to the universal dangers to a woman, and Feline protection customs, she was also aware, she did have a choice.

Well, he doesn't seem that bad a fellow, kind of endearing and lovable, if that's the way it must be. I sure wouldn't want to pick a bigger male. That Thor scares the bejebbies out of me.

The definite deciding factor was when they also educated her in medical procedures. Feather was euphoric; she had always wanted to be a healer. And to top off her delight, she found Uel to be a minor physician himself.

This life was a dream come true.

With her inclusion into the intimate nest of Dia, the owner of the huge med ship, Feather found, she could also be close to Susa, her hero in the universal field of curative medicine. Reassuringly, Feather would never be the solitary one of her kind in the nest. Reva had also been brought in by Thor; Steven with Amara and baby TaTa, were near at hand, as well, always there to converse with, share, complain to, and encourage her.

Her work appointment was to stay with the Noor female on the med floor. As Uel was the attendant to the large male Instant Healer, Loki, she was to be there to assist Susa. And always, there was Liam, who saw to the two Instant Healer's welfare, and guided the lesser attendants.

To observe the Instant Healers at work was fascinating; at times took her breath away, as Feather watched. When Susa touched a warrior's broken arm, it mended instantly. If Loki put his hand on the belly of a small Feline kitten, it started to purr, no longer in misery. But, the most terrifying aspect of their ability, was what it did to the Healer.

In seconds the condition or injury seemed to transfer to the physician, as if it were an infection. Feather, and Uel too, for he appeared as new at viewing the result as she; each would hold their breath, awaiting the full recovery of the one affected.

Oh, I once wanted healing powers such as these, but I never realized the real thing had such a cost.

And Susa, and that red headed male are so brave!

Feather just wished the two Healers weren't at odds with one another. It was obvious, Susa had something against the male. Every time he came even close to her, she would hiss like a snake about to strike. And Loki seemed to accept the condition, slinking away in apparent shame.

Why is she so mad at him? What has he done? If I didn't know better, I'd think she had met him before.

And then it dawned on Feather.

Can this be the one who has hurt her? But no! He's been here...on the ship...

They mentioned, Loki had been in prison...

Surely not Bom's prison?

Chapter 38

I've about had enough!

Every time Loki came near Susa, she hissed at him to move away; her back was up, figuratively, but nevertheless, she was very evidently not accepting the physical.

This is not good! Somehow, he is provoking her! And it stops right now!

Angrily, Liam grabbed Loki, and forcefully pulled him into the medical facility ante. The room was not only private, but sound proofed. Here the two could have it out without arousing interference from others.

With retribution on his mind, Liam shook Loki violently. When he stepped back, he had not eased his stance, merely given space for the further confrontation.

"What the devil is wrong with you, Loki?" Liam growled. "Why do you insist on infuriating my female. I've chosen her for us; she's a perfect match, but if you keep this up, you'll botch the whole thing."

Loki straightened his full eight foot three, five hundred and fifty pound massive frame in indignation. If he wanted, he could easily, physically, best his mental half. But, instead of fighting, he chose to challenge with words.

"Has she accepted you?" he asked evenly.

Not to be deterred, Liam quickly fired back. "She agreed to allow me promise..."

"Really? Does she know I am part of you?"

"She knows what we are! Now, she just needs to accept you, so we can go from there..."

"Have you shared mentally?"

"She knows my thoughts!" Liam declared testily. "I cannot hold her at bay. She is stronger than I. She knows everything!"

Loki laughed derisively. "But you, don't."

Liam frowned. "What do you mean by that? She's my future mate!" he exploded. "What's gotten into you since you've been in that prison? Let me into your mind; let me see, so I can heal you!"

"Heal me? You say mine, as if she was yours alone, and I have no place. She doesn't want me..."

"Are you jealous?" Liam demanded incredulously. "Aw, Loki...she will learn to care for you, too. Just be your nicer self..."

Loki howled with pent up frustration, anguish so palpable even Liam felt it. "She was mine first! I found her...before you!"

Liam's jaw dropped in shock.

"I've had her...physically!"

Liam gasped. He felt like he'd been punched in the belly. "Oh, golly," he said softly. "We are already...mated?"

Loki said nothing, only turned away as if shamed.

Then it dawned on Liam.

Loki was in Bom's prison...when Susa was there?

"Did you force her?" Liam hissed viciously.

"No," Loki returned quietly. "But...I was not wise...as you would have been. I was alone... without my mental...in a belt. I tried to think as you would."

Liam's heart melted. "Aw, Loki. Come here. We need to junction..."

But Loki still held back, reluctant. "No. I am...all wrong inside.

"She thinks I have rejected her. She is so angry with me...I thought I was doing what was best for her. I thought you had to find her first; to choose her. I couldn't tell you, because I thought it would influence your decision. Then it would be my doing; not yours, and...now she won't forgive me..."

"Let me in! Let me see," Liam pleaded softly. "We need to junction, Loki. Then we can figure out what to do."

"There's more," Loki admitted, still delaying. "Bom...will harm all of you, if I tell what went on in there."

"I already know what goes on down in his prison!" Liam hissed in disgust. "The three of us will deal with him when the opportunity arises."

"Four," corrected Loki.

"You know about the Essence?" Liam asked in surprise.

"Tilk? I made them."

"What!"

For the first time in a long time, Loki grinned.

As the two males touched hands, light flashed in the room, and instead of two beings, there was but one.

He was enormous, colossal, massive: nine feet tall, muscular and solid. His hair was now a combination of dark-silver and red-gold curls; the eyes were Feline, of turquoise with a bronze vertical slit center; the face, hands, and feet were still humanoid, but the ten foot sleek shorthaired tail was now like a shadow, barely visible.

Formidable! Indeed!

It is so wonderful; we are together at last!

As it should be.

And as one, each found the memories of the other, and...the needed wisdom.

Chapter 39

They are being way too nice...

Even though their physical appearance was still of two parts, it was like the Noor pair was now one individual. She knew Liam/Loki must have junctioned in private, for their every action, every thought seemed to harmonize with the other.

But this sudden, undivided attention toward her, petrified Susa. She was unprepared to handle such devotion. They were courting her...with all the fervor, and urgency, lost time had put into their hearts.

It shocked her; thrilled, and took her breath away. She felt almost smothered by their attention, their large size and close proximity, the emanating adoration. She was frightened out of her wits, had difficulty stringing two thoughts together sensibly.

Liam and Loki came up beside, one on either side of her, a gift in each pair of hands.

Liam went first, giving her a set of earrings: tiny, double, amethyst and turquoise butterflies, hanging, interlocking, one below the other. He placed them through her ears, with a gentle touch that made her shiver.

Then Loki held out a fragrant red carnation and placed it in her hair, just above her right ear, and when he stepped back, in his other hand, when he opened it, was a two inch square of maple fudge, her very favorite candy.

Tears brimmed in his eyes. "For my Tusha," he proclaimed shyly. "Loki, soo sorry..."

After he said that, Susa couldn't stay mad at him; it was the tears that were the deciding factor. She accepted his gifts.

****

After lunch, the males tested the waters again.

As the group left the dining area, Liam asked tentatively: "Will you join us for the walk back?" For a moment, Susa hesitated, then gave in.

Trailed by their constant shadows, Feather and Uel, as they entered the small corridor, between the med bay patient area and the pharmacy, Loki grew suddenly excited.

The Noor, as no other species, because of their exceedingly long life span, have a certain capacity for child-like behavior. Seldom do they allow it to show in public, but when it does exhibit, it is the physical male who is most susceptible; infrequently the mental succumbs. For both to yield at the same time, is totally unheard of.

Enthused by the thought of what appeared to be, at long last, his acceptance by Susa; Loki let out a jubilant yell, and lost control.

Shape-shifter that he was, his image rapidly shrunk, until he was the size of a large rodent. He had taken on the shape of a tiny, pesky creature found on many outer worlds, a cross between a marmot, and a hairless mole rat; an exceedingly ugly little beast, with a bushy tail, colorless naked body, buck teeth, sucker-like feet, and blind. Clearly, the depiction was meant in jest.

In an instant, Loki took off in this shape, speeding up the wall at the side of his companions, weaving back and forth across the ceiling, up and down the walls, like a rabid, frenzied animal, all the while squealing a challenge to his brother.

Susa stopped in startled astonishment.

It was no surprise, that his mental matching pair was also quickly affected. Liam almost instantly took up the dare, shape-shifting, as well, not changing much, but going for the full Feline shape, only much smaller, the size of a large tomcat; as if the two males had done this many times as young kits, often chasing each other.

****

Up the walls, over the ceiling, racing along the short corridor. For a second, Susa stayed where she was in stunned disbelief; then, as if she too caught the fever, she ran after the two males, to keep them in sight. She did not change shape as they did, only appeared to be enjoying their infantile behavior, like a mother watching over errant children.

Stunned at such extraordinary behavior by the normally restrained Noor Instant Healers, Uel and Feather stood still, holding their breath, awaiting what might happen next.

Beyond, in the pharmacy, they could see the free standing, many-level, glass-like, transparent, floor to ceiling shelves, containing drawers, over laden with glass vials and containers, filled with multi-colored liquids and powders.

When tiny, energetic, Loki reached this area, with his small cat-like brother chasing behind, and unthinkingly entered this disastrous abode, the two had retired to the floor. With horror, those watching realized the danger, but were shocked into inaction.

To add to the hazard, Kimon stood in the path of the speeding twosome. He turned abruptly, shocked surprise spreading across his face, as he realized what was coming. Apparently, experienced from past episodes in younger years, he growled in evident disapproval.

So, Loki headed up the wall.

The next step was inevitable. Considering the rapidity of the occurrence; and that the participants were in such an enraptured condition as to be oblivious, the intervention of an ordinary shout would never have penetrated their consciousness.

Nearly upon his smaller target, Liam mounted the wall, and as he passed, his body struck a corner of a shelf. In slow motion, the entire thirty foot span began to plummet toward the floor.

Almost at the same instant, all present heard Susa's mental command:

Liam! Loki! Stop! Go Normal!

And simultaneously, with an almost imperceptible wave of her hand, the tumbling shelves froze in midair, then were upright again, before the contents could hit and shatter on the floor.

The spectators released baited breath, as the two culprits, now at normal size and appearance, materialized to the left of Kimon. The Noor males turned toward the female that had both rescued them, and been inadvertently responsible for their unusual indiscretion.

Both Liam and Loki faded in embarrassment.

Kimon was livid!

"I thought you two had out grown such behavior?" Kimon thundered. "Are Noors in love cursed to never grow up?" As he seemed now to be talking to thin air, he bellowed the next command. "Show yourselves!"

The two males abruptly became visible.

"You're too big to be scruffed...and too old," Kimon reasoned. "What punishment do you think appropriate?"

The guilty pair simply hung their heads.

Almost timidly, Susa broke in. "It was my fault..."

Kimon spun on her; hissed disapproval.

"Males in our species are taught self-control from infancy. They have no excuse for this!"

"It was still...because of me..."

"In our society, we do not blame the female! Most definitely, we will not hold responsible...one such as you..."

"Then, I entreat you, Kimon," Susa pleaded. "Let this go. The harm was prevented, and...I don't think such an occurrence will happen again."

For a second he stood silently debating; then he grunted, and turning away, dismissed them.

Sheepishly, the two males continued on their way, with Susa between them; Uel and his mate quietly following.

Feather could not help but marvel at the unspoken dominance, Susa seemed to have over the cantankerous old Head Physician.

****

"Whew! That was close," muttered Loki.

Liam chuckled. "I wouldn't have allowed him to scruff you," he declared quietly.

"I saw in his mind," Loki admitted. "He wanted to put me in a cage...wearing a drain belt." He shivered visibly. "A tiny cage...too small to fit me. I know, if that ever occurred, I'd go to madness quite quickly...it is a great weakness of mine: fear of enclosed spaces..."

"I won't ever let that happen, Physical," Liam once again reassured. "They would have to kill me first!"

"Keep me in line, next time, Liam," Loki pleaded. "I am the unstable one...too much empathy sense."

"You need that to heal. I will keep watch over you...keep you out of trouble..."

"And who will maintain your balance, mind-male?" Susa asked pointedly.

Liam grinned, and shrugged. "Why...you, of course."

"I see. So, I am to police you two?"

"And, we, you," Liam agreed. "That's how our union works. But police is rather harsh; help and guide is more adequate...as you just did."

Chapter 40

In the home nest, at the evening meal, Susa was again the beleaguered female. Now that Loki felt accepted, both males wished to serve her. Sitting on either side of her, neither would eat, until they felt her needs were adequately met; and, they insisted upon sharing the choicest morsels from their plates.

Susa hadn't been afraid of Loki in the prison; he'd never been anything but gentle to her. Nor had she feared Liam when they had been together in the Earth forest compound. But now, with the two together surrounding her, as if they were sentinels to protect her against the outside world, she felt threatened. Compared to her diminutive size, they seemed colossal. Instead of experiencing comfort at their proximity, she was overwhelmed by a feeling of smothered panic.

A second factor added to her dilemma. Each time Loki touched, memories of other times flooded back. Her skin tingled, her breath came quick; warmth spread from her belly to her breasts. Her physical body was responding to him; it was extremely difficult to keep her need at bay.

I cannot trust him. If I give in to my wants, he'll betray me again. Like the last time...when trials overwhelmed.

What Susa failed to take into account was that now it was different with Liam a part of the equation.

Oblivious to her quandary, Loki finally slipped behind her. To him, it was quite natural; he had done it this way in their prison apartment, when she was too weak and tired to sit comfortably. He meant to support, like a chair behind, drawing her to his lap, his arms encircling her. It had been a pleasure to feed her so intimately; he merely wanted to experience once again, what they had as patient and physician. But, this was now, more a love gesture, no longer simply a caregiver's tenderness.

It had been why she so often had hissed him away, afraid of close contact. Now, she could no longer do that, for she feared to break his spirit.

Loki sensed her tension at his touch, but ignored it, assuming it was due to their long time apart. Each time she accepted a choice morsel, Susa felt pressured, dominated; she dreaded the future.

And Tilk seemed no help at all. It appeared as if she had gone to sleep, simply allowing the physical parts of each pair to work it out together. When Susa probed for her input, the mind person, for some unknown reason, only focused her anger on their physical body.

After the meal, when all the family had settled in to watch a video together, Susa began to tremble visibly.

I can't hold it together much longer! I need to get out of here!

"I need...I need," Susa stuttered, quickly rising to her feet. "I need...to be alone...please!"

I need space! I need to let it out! To sort it out! The males think the problem solved, but it isn't!

Susa had yet to completely surrender.

"Okay," agreed the junction males in unison.

****

It was as easy as that!

Susa fled through the side door, on the inner wall of the main communal sleep/activity area, into the recreation center beyond.

Where to go? I need a place like my grotto.

In her mind, she searched the plans of the ship. In the very center of the huge transport was a large park, formed for the pleasure of all inhabitants aboard.

Yes! Park! It will serve.

She needed to vent, and balance her feelings.

****

Feather had recognized the terror in the Noor female's eyes. She'd seen it only once before, but she would never forget the results she had witnessed. She knew what was about to happen.

She arose from her place in Uel's arms, and moved quickly over to the two Noor giants. Deliberately, Feather blocked Liam's view of the huge wall screen.

"Are you two dense, or what?" she demanded.

Dia immediately hissed disapproval; Uel cringed, expecting the worst, but Feather was not to be deterred.

"Do you have any idea what she's about to do?" she went on. "I've watched what she does to get her head on straight..."

At her words, she felt the probe of Liam's mind in her own. Feather gasped at the sudden intrusion, but it wasn't painful, simply unexpected, and then the Noor mind was gone again, as abruptly as he had entered.

"Spit!" Liam swore. "Come on, Loki!" he ordered, rising swiftly, pulling his twin to his feet with him.

And then the two vanished into thin air.

****

They were able to surprise her only because she was in such a state she had shut down her defenses.

In one huge fist, Loki caught Susa up by the back of her blouse, suspending her roughly above the pathway. She twisted, hissing like a she-cat, clawing at empty air, her weapon-claws fully extended.

Liam stayed at a safe distance, holding her mental powers at bay, so the physical male had a chance to deal with the irate physical little spitfire. Because Susa had been caught off guard, Tilk was sluggish to come to her rescue. The mind male could keep her down, because she too had been mired in anger, and slow to come to the surface.

Loki let Susa fight ineffectively until she seemed to play out. He was about to set her down, when Liam cautioned telepathically.

She's faking!

Instead, the huge Physical suddenly crushed her close against his chest, and held her tight. Susa was mentally strong, which gave her body added strength, but even so, she was not strong enough to fight up close, against the formidable strength of the powerful unmatched Loki.

After a time, he demanded ominously in a low voice: "You ready to listen, now?"

Against his chest, she went limp, nodded.

"What you plan is not the way to handle your needs!"

Tears of defeat and frustration spilled down her cheeks, wetting the front of his garment, but as yet he did not trust her not to flee again, and continued to hold her close.

Liam stepped forward cautiously, touched Loki's arm, and jumped them to the Noor private running track, where they would be less public. Here they could argue...or fight unseen.

Loki finally set her down between them.

"We run, now?" Loki asked hopefully.

At the manhandling, her anger quickly resurfaced. She turned, and took off in a flash.

As they sped after her, the fleet footed Loki in the lead, both males were relieved she hadn't thought to teleport beyond their reach. Each had the same thought:

Wow! Can she ever run!

****

They must have done a hundred laps, of the mile long circular track, and still they hadn't caught her. Suddenly, Susa simply dropped in her tracks.

When the males reached her side, she was in a fainting stupor. Remorseful, Loki gently gathered her in his arms, and cuddled her close.

After a time, when she began to show more alertness, Loki began to talk quietly to her. Liam sat to the side, like a supervisor. He told himself:

This is between the Physicals; I am not needed.

"I have gone over and over our beginning days," Loki confided to Susa. "I will never be washed free of my guilt. I have hurt you far too much...to ever be forgiven..."

Susa began to cry, tears running unchecked, coursing ever faster down her pale cheeks, until she sobbed with total lack of control.

"I love you beyond measure," Loki went on. "I will love you forever. And if ever I hurt you again, Liam can pound the fecal matter out of me."

Through her tears, she began to laugh uncontrollably, struck by the mental image such an attempt conjured up. Loki's sober face began to show the first dawning of hope.

"I should not need it," he said sadly. "But I do...I need...I need...you...to..."

"I do love you, Loki!" Susa said, going directly to the source of the problem. "Sometimes, perceived rejection turns love...to hate. I am the one who should apologize...I am sorry..."

When the tears began again to overflow, Loki kissed them away.

At last, Liam moved forward to join them. And Susa was okay with the closeness of both males, now that the barriers had been broken down.

****

When Loki carried her into the room, it was obvious to all, that Susa had been crying. She hid her face against his shoulder, and he seemed to be enjoying the intimate touch of her smooth skin.

Grinning from ear to ear, like a Cheshire cat that had just swallowed a mouse, Liam looked as if he'd been given a delightful morsel at an anticipated feast.

Dia was immediately in protective mode. "Where have you two been all this time? And what have you been doing?"

"Running, momma," Loki replied, tongue-in-cheek. "Susa can beat me!"

Dia growled. "You'd better not have hurt her..."

Almost simultaneously, Kimon barked a laugh. "Found someone to put you in your place at last, did you?"

Liam chuckled. "More or less..."

Dia harrumphed. "Well...time for bed, then!"

That night Susa allowed both males to come close; Liam in front; Loki behind. She looked like a small coddled teen between her two giant protectors. And apparently, none was cold, nor had trouble sleeping.

****

Just before they settled down themselves, Feather whispered to Uel.

"Which one do you suppose Susa will choose? Or is it permitted for her to have two husbands?"

Uel chuckled softly. "You do not comprehend the facts, female. The Junction is one unit."

"Junction? What is that?"

"Liam/Loki; they are one combined unit."

"But which one is it? Which is this Junction?"

Uel gave a frustrated hiss.

"Both. The Junction is...okay, like this...they are two halves...they belong together. Liam is mind; Loki the body..."

"Eh, what?" She turned to face him.

Uel grinned. "Shh...others will hear."

Feather went silent, waiting for more.

"Once, I also found it hard to grasp. I have never seen them combine; very few have, but they tell me the completed being is much larger, and very, very formidable. That is why they remain separated; for the ease of those around them...we would become too fearful..."

"Susa's two fellows are one...being?"

"They are not two; only one."

"Man! That's hard to wrap your head around, especially since they look like two separate guys..."

Uel pulled in behind Feather, easing her closer against him, but just before he began to settle down into drowsy stupor, she asked one last question.

"But, why did Susa fight Loki?"

"I can only surmise," Uel stated. "I think...they were already mated...I...and another from the prison...were responsible. But...that is a story for another time."

"But," persisted Feather. "Why was she so angry at him, then?"

"He...when he was released, he did not take her with him. He couldn't...Bom ordered him to leave her behind; meant to kill her, as soon as he was gone. But, Loki tricked him, and set her free, instead."

"Ah." Feather realized the crux of the matter. "She took it as rejection...and that hurts!"

"He suffered much...as well," Uel vehemently defended.

"But..." Feather declared, closing her eyes at last. "Now, they have made up."

Like a reader having finished a love story with a good ending, she sighed happily, as if the peace between the Noor couple made all right in her world, also.

****

Feline hearing is very acute. If the young pair thought their conversation only for themselves, they were wrong. Those who had been listening, Feline, Noor, and human alike, smiled to themselves, as they settled down. The nest was indeed in harmony, once again.

When all were finally quiet, Kimon purred in his mate's ear:

"All ends well, after all."

Dia's murmur of assent was barely audible.

Chapter 41

A few nights later, Loki awoke in the middle of the sleep period. His Tusha had turned toward him, her back to Liam. Both she, and his Mental, were wide awake, as well.

It was her velvet hand caressing sensuously over his chest, that had brought Loki to full awareness. The delicate appendage travelled seductively across his generous pectorals, arousing him to enthusiasm.

Liam teleported the three to a place more private.

On a warm sunny planet much like Earth, but of a hotter and brighter environment, and closer to that foreign sun, they slowly materialized. Though the journey had taken but a moment, it had cooled the immediate passions, so they could think more clearly.

The two males stepped away. They stood in verdant grasses, beyond a muted waterfall. The trees were in flower; bearing fruit, as well. In the distance, shining domed structures of brilliant silver stood, as if awaiting the arrival of one thought forever lost. This was the Noor ancestral world, and none had been here, since Tilk had been captured.

A barrier surrounded the planet, impeding all enemy, as well as friend, from entering without authorization. None emerged to welcome or turn away; the world appeared devoid of populace.

The two males touched hands to junction, becoming as one single being, for here there was no one to become alarmed, or to fear. The female was not panicked by their outsized appearance; she had known, and accepted, what they were; expected it.

Tilk/Susa grew to match his size.

Hand in hand, the two proceeded, along the shore of a pleasant, tree shaded pond, until they were beside the thundering cascade, and came upon a crystal cave, with walls bright and luminous, just behind the water sheet. They entered.

It was as if this grotto had been prepared for just such a venture as they planned. The floor of the cave was spread with rich colorful tapestry; flower petals were spread across the blankets; bowls of fruit, and flasks of drink awaited consumption. It was as if time stood frozen at the last time the space had been used.

Gently, Liam/Loki eased his female to the mat. His caress was gentle, loving, careful; his kisses like wine, arousing a hunger inside her. She matched him in fervor, until flesh joined flesh in intimacy.

Their frenzied activity proceeded until the figures involved began to glow intensely. When they had reached a force beyond the vision of mere man, the transparent image of Tilk became a separate form. She was the exact reproduction of the beautiful Susa.

Now that there were two females, the males divided also.

Still luminous, physical paired off with mental: Liam to Susa; Tilk and Loki.

The glow intensified as the pairs were mating, until...all were invisible.

At some point, exhaustion overcame, and the figures could be seen again, entwined in each other's arms, in a pod formation, smaller female between the two giant males, asleep.

They awoke slowly, nourished each other from the bountiful supply at hand, and fondly repeated their love making. Needless to say, time had no meaning in their new found affection for each other.

****

Kimon moved into the doorway of the communication workroom. All eyes turned his way.

"Where ever is Susa...and the junction males?" he asked fretfully. "I haven't seen them all day."

He was eldest male present of the Noor Susa clan, so it fell upon Shiveron to answer.

"No Instant Healers available for a while," he stated bluntly.

"Why?" Kimon demanded.

"They are busy," Nyle said cryptically.

For a moment, Kimon stood uncomprehending. At last, the truth dawned upon him.

"Oh...well..." he said in embarrassment. "I guess, we'll have to do without them." Then he turned on his heel, and left abruptly.

As the head physician disappeared out onto the floor again, Thor let out a chuckle.

"Now," he declared, as someone considerably experienced with the individual in question. "That was totally unlike him. With anyone else, he'd be storming mad at not being told in advance."

Nyle grinned impishly. "My mother has a way with him..." he observed simply.

****

For three days they were not seen on the med ship, and one quiet afternoon, when the Noor female, and her junction pair, did put in an appearance, the usual harried expression to her face had softened. Now, she smiled a lot, a shy dreamy smile that melted your heart.

It was clear by their loving attention toward each other, they were deeply in love. They worked in tandem, anticipating each other's needs. When not needed for the work they were doing, their hands were constantly touching, soothingly caressing the back of the other. Susa would cuddle against the chest of her Physical; the Mental would unabashedly reach out and stroke her silken curls.

And so the days flew by. Those around the three were so much encouraged at the love shown by the Noor , that they too found gentle gestures, and caring attitudes, easy to display toward their own appointed partners.

Chapter 42

The day came Liam/Loki was summoned to present his mate to his foster grandmother.

They went the conventional way, using the jump portal on the med ship, to Jump center, and then, to the large central planet of government in the Feline system. After some difficulty going through security, they were at last ushered into the presence of Kei, the Feline Queen.

The door closed behind the last of her guardians, for Kei had expressly forbidden any warrior to remain, insisting she was safe in the protection of her grandsons. The silence was heavy; the Noor each felt a bubbling anger in the breast of the small Feline before them.

Her silver fur was streaked with white; body old and frail, but her regal manner was evident still, as she reclined on her lavish couch.

It was obvious Kei had been briefed on all circumstances. With an inbred dignity, she turned to address Susa.

"Know you, female," Kei demanded, coming immediately to her purpose. "How these, my grandsons, and other half Noor, were conceived?"

"I have viewed all documentation available about the Noor, but the actual conception process was not in the data."

"And you have not probed for the information?"

"No, my lady. I am reluctant to invade the thoughts of a Monarch such as you."

"Good. Then you are ignorant of what I am about to disclose." With a wave of her paw, Kei motioned them to seat themselves. "Do not read me now either," she instructed. "Allow me the privilege of telling it verbally, for it has not been for public knowledge to this point. I will pass it to you with the hope you will consider it private, as well. I, and those of Dia's Noor nest, are the only ones privy to these facts."

Kei paused, collecting her thoughts, as if preparing to relive an unpleasant experience. Susa gave her the privacy she desired, choosing not to preview what was coming.

"I was sent this vision from their Noor mother. I know it is fact, because we found the boys exactly where she said."

The Feline Queen took a ragged breath. Clearly, she did not like telling the tale.

"It is Roog habit to torture both Feline and Noor, but some time ago, by chance, they stumbled on a more heinous method of torment than any before it. Normally, they merely enjoy watching drugged up male Feline fight to protect their females..."

Kei closed her eyes, and shivered visibly. Susa could feel her revulsion; the fear of the deadly dominate creatures.

"When the Roog dogs were seeking to annihilate the peaceful Noor beings, they amused themselves with something they call rape/torture. It was their practice to drain a Noor female of her essence power to the point of semi-consciousness; just at the verge of death. They then tied an unconscious male of another species to her. As both were allowed to regain consciousness, they were injected with a cocktail of powerful stamina enhancing drugs laced with arousal properties..."

Susa gasped, as she realized where this was going. She wasn't sure she wanted to hear more, but Kei continued hurriedly, wanting to get done with her appalling account.

"When the Noor female half awakens, she is in desperate need. The pheromones she secrets render any male unable to resist; this is how she seduces her partner when she needs him, but she responds to none but her own mate. She gives off a static charge that instantly kills, if another tries to take her.

"With most other species, the male is simply incinerated; fried to a crisp. But...the beastly Roog realized, a Feline has a defensive trick. If a male senses his female is dying, he will mate to her to raise her stamina. In this case, the dogs decided to use it against them.

"Long before the protective Noor reflex can be produced, the Feline male has sensed the need, and acts upon it. The body temperature of a Noor female reaches extremes while mating. And of course, the result is the same..."

Kei pursed her lips in a hard line. "We have always prided ourselves on the self-control we teach our young, but when the male is highly drugged, he does not know what he is doing... anymore, than the Noor female realizes what is happening. This amuses the Roog...and humiliates us. Most times, the rape produces no offspring...we have only found a rare few...and have tried to protect them. Even some of my own people have been against us for this, because they are uninformed. I sought to protect them from the gruesome facts...perhaps I am wrong."

"To make this public knowledge, would begin an all out war against the Roog," Susa observed.

Kei nodded. "You understand, then. The Feline are a timid species, but vengeful war is not beyond us. We would be guilty of genocide, just as the Roog."

She sighed. "So, now...I must tell you the rest."

Kei looked away, and Susa noted a change in her demeanor. She was now more shamed, then anything else.

"My successor was to come through my last living male cousin, but...when he was still in his prime, before he could be mated, he was captured by Roog. For many years, we had no idea of his whereabouts. Then one day, I was shown the vision of his death, and...told by the dying Noor female, where to find the son he had propagated.

"When we sent the rescue unit, the crew was surprised to find two. In the interval between mother's leaving, and the arrival of our ship, the junction males had learned to separate. We assume their mother educated them by a delayed process, which gave them the knowledge when the need arose. As the future was to unfold, they would shock and terrify us many times, when they discovered new abilities. Because of that fear, I think they learned more to hide from us, than trust."

Liam grinned, and nodded agreement.

"Liam/Loki was the first. I appointed my best friend, Dia, to nurture them. And as we found the others, we sought to protect them from public view...and discrimination.

"But Clio, that dog, head of the Universal council, began to spread the rumor, that being Noor was a virus contamination. Suddenly, many began to fear any association with those of Noor blood; some creatures, to this very day, still have that attitude...that Noor are inferior. The decree was passed, that they may not mate, except among themselves, and they were never to be permitted young. But we did try to counteract, by leaking data about Noor benevolence, and their history."

Kei looked to Susa. "And now, dear, I am certain you have surmised the rest. Would you like to state the obvious?"

Susa let the silence ride a moment; then she answered with a question.

"As your cousin was to produce the heir to your throne, just how does the monarchy progress?"

"As you know, the Feline are ruled by a female. It has always been so," Kei admitted. "If the heir is a male, we either wait for the next born female, or...the mate of the heir becomes ruler..."

Tilk/Susa said nothing. She wanted it spoken by the present Monarch.

"I am to judge the worthiness of my successor," Kei finally declared. "In my opinion, the Queen of the Noor race is supremely qualified to be sovereign of the Feline peoples. I would gladly abdicate to you."

Susa closed her eyes, forcefully driving away the old panic that rose to the surface, unwanted. She stated her attitude, bluntly.

"You place me at a disadvantage; dual Monarchy; double trouble... The Noor beings, I can handle; we are small, but twelve planets with fifty trillion each! Help! And I see in your mind, it won't end there. You have the idea, I will also, one day, rule the Universe..."

"That is the Noor prophesy..."

Annoyed, Susa frowned. "My essence must have been inebriated, when she predicted that! I come from the Forbidden Planet. My people are the most undisciplined, aggressive humans in the Universe!"

"Where do you think I came from, dear? I was born a slave, in the belly of the Slither system...creatures with no feelings raised me; yet I am...cat!"

Susa shivered, then laughed. "Aw, well...you are not yet dead, dear Kei..."

And then a most disconcerting vision of the near future assaulted her senses.

"You...have, reached the end of your days..."

Kei nodded. "I too see..." she stated softly.

Liam moaned. "Not yet," he challenged.

"Not just yet," Kei agreed. "But we need to prepare... Today, I hand over the reins of the Feline nation. Rule well, young one."

Calmly, Susa took command. "May I ask one small favor in this transition?"

"You are now Feline Queen. All must obey your every whim."

"Will you be proxy...carry on as if you were still Queen?"

Kei agreed. "Gladly. Are your wishes then, for things to carry on as before?"

"Yes. Except...what of the Universal council?"

"You sit as member representative of the Feline species; second chair to Clio..."

"And how does one unseat head chair?"

"Clio can only be removed through a trial before the Universal court, in which he is indisputably convicted of a grievous crime toward a developing race, or the destruction of one...aw," she said in sudden understanding. "You have proof?"

Susa nodded. "I want you to begin setting that process in motion. And...also, only record our transition of power in the Feline data bank. The fact is to be kept secret for the moment, even from our own people."

"So our hand may not be disclosed prematurely..." Kei nodded. "Excellent! You are our hidden weapon!"

Kei enfolded Susa in her frail arms. As the two withdrew from the embrace, Kei had one last thing to say.

"I fear," she sighed. "We shall never meet face to face again. It saddens me...we have only just met."

Susa did not contradict Kei's assessment; she couldn't lie. After all, she was Noor.

Epilogue:

Susa snuggled luxuriously back against Loki's warm body behind her. His head rested against her shoulder; hers was on Liam's chest. As a pea in a pod, so they slept always now. Comfortable. Yet...something was wrong.

What woke me?

The room seemed much darker than usual.

As a precaution, to ensure their safety, all Noor had been outfitted with headbands, and energy belts like the ones Susa had first made for herself on her old home world. During the day, they were worn, but at night the belts felt too cumbersome to sleep in, so each removed them, and set them aside. It left them vulnerable during rest periods; but, they reasoned, there was always at least two guardians on constant alert outside the residence, and the many Feline about them for protection.

Also, in Dia's sleep quarters, the ceiling was energized with a specific type of energy to supply Noor needs, and even when the exterior light was dimmed, the energy continued, visible only to the mental eyes of a sensitive Noor.

The energy source has gone out!

Susa became aware of a pungent odor to the room, like the burning of electric wires. Her body began to tingle in a most uncomfortable way.

Eyes turned from blue to rainbow hues; Tilk came thundering to the surface.

Memory of another time fled passed the vision of the Mental: these same feelings, just before the attack and capture.

Danger!!!

Tilk had no time; she could not escape to the safety of the headband, as they had done when Bom had turned the laser weapon upon them in the dungeon prison. Then, they had come prepared; now they were not. It was already too late, and this weapon was much larger, encompassing the entire area.

Abruptly, the mind...and body, shut down.

Oblivion!

****

Sometime later, Thor jerked awake with a start. He could still smell a drug in the air. Around him, Feline, Bear, and human alike, were stirring from muddled stupor, holding their heads, as if in pain.

Something is very wrong!

That's when the eldest male Feline realized, the bed nest was empty of every last Noor. One or two might leave for a romantic encounter, and they would never take the young ones with them. Neither would they all go at once.

Thor rose up, spitting with anger.

I have failed in my pledge to protect them!

"Alert! Alert!" he screamed, pounding at the inter-ship communicator on the wall. "The ship contains intruders! The air is filled with poison. Close off the circulation vents! Flush the system!"

Thor turned to the head physician, who was slowly rising. Being smaller, he had most likely ingested more than others.

"Kimon!"

The male moaned; was sluggish. Dia appeared more alert.

"Check on the warriors," she ordered. "How did this happen? How could we have been caught so off guard?"

It was then she noted the absence of her Noor children. She screamed like a banshee, and after that, no one could console her.

It was the males who took over command, the reorganization of personal. The return response should have been instant, but all over the ship, for the longest while...there was silence.

Disjointedly, gradually, groggy voices answered: one young male was missing from the pilot section; he had been a trainee; one of Dia's own immediate relatives.

Surely, Tza is no traitor. I handpicked him myself.

But the most disconcerting thought was more:

Where are the Noor? Do the Roog have them? All of them?

###

Guide to knowing the creatures of this tale:

NOOR: a humanoid being with exceptional psychic abilities, the degree varying with each individual. Some also have the capability to separate its mental essence from the physical body.

-In a conjunctive male: the two halves exhibit themselves as two separate physical entities.

example: Liam/Loki

-In an introvert female: the two display as different personalities; only one dominates at a time.

example: Tilk/Susa.

FELINE: man-size intelligent cat beings.

example: Dia, Kimon, Uel

BEAR: a giant bear being-intelligent, protective, used as body guards

ROOT: tree-like beings. Said to have little empathy, a trickster and devious.

example: Theee, More and Zaba

ROOG: large dog-like beings. Not necessarily highly intelligent; very aggressive and predatory.

SLITHER: snake-like creature with chameleon abilities. Also able to remain invisible for long periods of time. Usually a light blue-green, but color darkens when they are about to attack. Only emotions it is capable of are protective instinct and anger-attack. When a Slither emotionally attaches to a being not of their kind, it will protect for life.

BOM: a cross-breed Roog/Feline

LIAM/LOKI: a cross-breed Noor/Feline

Other NOOR/FELINE are: Twila and Jabek; Shiveron and Reon

TUSHA: a HUMAN/NOOR-(tusha is the name for butterfly in the Noor tongue)

Other HUMAN/NOOR: Nyle and Kaudy, Moriah and Iora.

SLITHER/HUMAN: Sith and mate Serene

BEAR/HUMAN: Wadi and mate Rimu

About the Author:

Margaret Afseth, a Canadian novelist, grew up on the prairies. She raised her four children from preschool age to teens on her own. Now, as a widow and grandmother, through the encouragement of her family to follow her dream of writing full time, and publishing her work, she has stepped to the publishing stage in the latter years of her life.

Since her late teens, Margaret was always an avid reader and clandestine writer, but due to discouragement, and the unfortunate hard lesson in which her first novel was destroyed by a misguided counselor, she was too publisher shy to go through the gauntlet of the critics...until, that is, the ease of on line self-publishing became available.

In February 2013 Margaret published her first sci-fi thriller the Aopato Chronicles.

Discover other titles by Margaret Afseth at
Amazon.com

Aopato book 1 (Aopato Chronicles)
Remedy book 2 (Aopato Chronicles)
Turn Back book 3 (Aopato Chronicles)
Gentle Beast-book 1 (Noor Chronicles)

If you enjoyed this book, here is a sample of book three of the Noor Chronicles; coming soon:

HEALER NEST
By
Margaret Afseth

PROLOGUE:

With the help of a sleep teaching disk, Bom upgraded his education in computer board programs, and noxious substances. He already was sufficiently familiar with advanced Roog weaponry.

His diminutive personal ship was completely automated. He knew enough of its operation to take it alone into deep space, through Jumper Central, and reach any destination in a matter of days. And though he could not operate it, the bay of his ship also contained a fair sized shuttle for his convenience.

Approaching Dia's enormous city-size emergency treatment facility was exceptionally easy. Bom was a registered Feline, even though he was half Roog; of a race that was their mortal enemy. But, the system simply accepted him.

As yet, they have not blocked me, though that will certainly change after this night's actions. But, by then, what I wish to accomplished will be done, I will be long gone, and it will no longer matter.

Uncontested, he slid his mini ship into a dock in the cavernous bay, and hit the image on his screen to power down.

As soon as he entered the med ship proper, Bom went straight to their mainframe. Most were on sleep break, which meant a skeleton staff. No one challenged him.

He went in with the password he'd set up from an outside terminal. It was in his father's name, who supposedly had access to all and any data, in any frame, because of his station as head of the Universal council.

It was easy to shut down inter-ship communications, and drop the shields on Dia's home nest. Even her Slither sentries were unaware of the change, that their charges were now vulnerable to outside attack.

Then he introduced the canister of the powerful sedative, he'd brought with him from his ship; fed it directly into the ventilation system, and donned an artificial breather.

After waiting the allotted time for the drug to take effect, he shut down the Noor energy ceiling in Dia's sleep room. Remotely, Bom blanketed the area with the drain beam weapon aboard his ship.

The whole thing went so well. The corridor door opened easily to his touch. When he arrived at the chamber, the Slither guards were visible, unconscious on the floor.

Using medic drones, who were programmed with the code for an emergency, he easily entered the sanctum of Dia, and transported the incapacitated Noor to his docked ship.

But, he had taken too long. Even though his prisoners were now shackled, and in drain belts, with a drain beam blanketing the compartment where they were held, he never knew what Loki's she was capable of.

And, he had one more need to fill.

I need a shuttle pilot! For that last distance to the moon cavern, I can't use the jump portal. Too many hostages now. Never knew they had accumulative so much family! And I only took those with the headbands...

Bom strode through the silent corridors of the single-warrior sleep-chambers, searching for one who would fit his criteria. There was no time left to pick and choose among these unconscious occupants.

Can't be certain, the one I pick, can operate a shuttle...

And, someone might awaken, and discover what he had done.

At just that moment the intercom sounded.

I must have missed a backup system!

"Alert! Alert!" came Thor's angry voice. "The ship contains intruders! The air is filled with poison. Close off the circulation vents! Flush the system!"

Enough of this! I need one of the captain's crew!

Bom spun on his heel, and headed at a lope, for the nearest lift. He hoped they wouldn't be clear thinking enough to shut those down just yet.

On the upper deck, the mixed breed creature found the slumped, still unconscious figures of five Feline minor officers; one was a skinny, pure white, long haired, younger male, perhaps, in his late twenties, obviously an apprentice. But Bom knew, if he was on the command deck, they had already trained him to operate both the larger vessel, as well as a shuttle.

He'll not have had much practice, but...he'll have to do.

And...he should stay out for a bit longer. He's not so large...will have ingested more of the drug.

Slinging the unfortunate trainee to his shoulder, Bom took off hurriedly to the down elevator, descending rapidly to the bowels, where his ship was docked.

****

At the age of two thousand and one, Kei needed her many naps more so than any other Feline in the species. She awoke now, instantly alert, blinking fearfully, panic coursing through her system.

She had had a most terrifying vision!

Kei had dreamed: that the Noor Queen, and all her clan, had been incarcerated; the one she'd chosen to take her place would now never head the twelve Feline planets, nor rescue the Universe from the rule of the devil dogs. The plight of all was sealed by order of Clio, the Roog head of the Universal council, and his mixed breed son, Bom. With all the Noor in captivity, there was no one to thwart the desires of these two bestial foes.

The Feline proxy ruler trembled, her body shaking visibly.

It can't be true. I won't believe it! It was merely a nightmare, brought on by undigested food.

Besides, if such a thing has happened, the end result is not a done deal. The Maker of us all has plans for her. It will not let it end like this!

****

The atmosphere of the middle world, in the twelve planet system, seemed suddenly to hold its breath. Then abruptly space split, and the area about the enormous globe was filled with enemy ships, materializing as if from thin air. Huge monster battle craft, resembling the dogs that piloted them, surrounded the seat of Feline government on all sides.

But this region is said to be protected! How did they slipped into Feline space, so close and undetected? Had they stolen the technology from the very peoples they were now threatening? Who betrayed the Feline species?

Bom? Or his father, Clio?

****

A male sentry, the fated messenger, risking his own death, burst into the sacrosanct chambers of his Monarch. The huge guardian warrior, beside the cot where she reclined, turned, on instant alert, claws extended, spitting viciously.

"Easy," the old female warned, sitting up. "Stand down! Give him time; he means me no harm."

Then waving for the panting intruder to come forward, she addressed him.

"What is the meaning of this unscheduled entry into my presence? Your message had best be of vital importance, or I will let my protector have at you."

"My Lady," he gasped. "The planet is surrounded by enemy ships...the dogs..."

Kei did not wait for another word. She turned to the warrior at her side.

"Summon the superintendent of evacuation...No!" she decided, abruptly changing her mind, as she realized there was too little time. "Tell him...begin to transport the females, their partners, and their families to other safe systems. He is to use all available jump portals, and to proceed with the utmost haste. We need to save as many as possible..."

"You must be the first, my Lady," ventured her guardian. But she immediately disagreed.

"Their purpose in choosing this planet first, is to cut off the head, so that the limbs will be without direction, and therefore, they think, useless. But, as always, they have underestimated us. I am ruler no longer...only the proxy."

Stunned, the two males present looked at her speechless for a second.

"My Lady?" finally ventured the one who had so rudely burst in. "What say you?"

"The Monarchy has been passed to my successor some time ago. She wished me to remain as proxy, as a means of deception, and it has worked. Now that the Roog have finally shown their hand, I see it as a wise decision. But, to the matter at hand. Why do you hesitate? Lives are in the balance!"

As her guardian went to the computer wall board to carry out her wishes, the one who remained behind probed further:

"But Lady. Where then is our real Sovereign?"

Kei smiled. "Pass the word, young warrior. The twelve planets are not crippled, even should I die. You will all know, when you find the one you seek. Use your logic; and it is on record... fight now! We are at war with the devil dogs! Protect the real Queen!"

"But you, my Lady. What will become of you?"

"I am old; I have lived a long and delightful life. I will not regret my passing...go, young one. Leave me, now."

****

Tzachok opened his blue eyes with great difficulty. It seemed in their lack of focus, he was seeing double.

"So, you are finally awake," growled a deep voice.

Tza yelped when he could finally see the huge form crouched before him. Even as a young kit, the half dog creature had frightened him, and he would run and hide, leaving his elders to deal with Bom.

The small Feline gagged at the odor that reeked off his subjugator's body, for the mixed breed male was none too clean. He was not inclined to wash his fur, as other Feline did. Nor was he pleasant to look at, either.

His bulldog-like visage was pure canine, a dark black with tan markings. The ears flopped over, instead of standing up, and were rounded at the ends, unlike the pointy ears of other Feline. His features resembled his Roog father, Clio, and like him, he had the vicious predatory nature.

But, his body was that of a cat; long black course fur, matted bushy tail, and deadly claws.

Bom stood up, his heavy build and eight foot height towering menacingly.

"Well, get up! I have work for you to do."

Tza swallowed convulsively. He knew there was no point trying to fight this beast, so he followed submissively after him.

Bom led him to the controls of a shuttle.

"Fly me down to the surface."

The younger Feline took his seat.

As they escaped the bay of the larger ship, Tza found he was nowhere near home. Far away he saw a blue and green planet; one he'd often seen on the simulator screen, for they used the Forbidden planet as the target in all training.

Oh, Almighty Maker, am I going to Bom's dungeon prison? What have I done to deserve this?

But Bom interrupted his thoughts. "Steer us to the dark side of its moon."

Tza breathed a sigh of relief.

Perhaps there is hope, after all.

But as he came around to the valley on the dark side, in closer to the surface, there beneath him was a cavernous holding bay, leading into the bowels of the rock. He landed, and powered down.

Tzachok thought his job was over now, but Bom was not yet finished with him.

"Come; we have to hurry, before they wake up on me."

When Tza saw the prisoners, in the shuttle's holding cells, his spirit plummet drastically. Bom had all members of the mighty Healer clan, even the youngest female, Kaudy, in torture drain-belts, and shackle chains. Hand and foot, they were hobbled, near bent double, so they couldn't move; still unconscious, and drained of energy. The mighty Noor were helpless, and there was nothing he could do to set them free.

Tza began to keen in fearful dread of the fate that awaited them.

"Shut up!" bellowed Bom, cuffing him alongside the head. "What good are you, if you are going to whine like that?"

The young Feline went to his knees, sobbing uncontrollably.

"If I didn't need your help, I'd end your miserable life right now, you poor excuse of a cat moron!" Then it seemed to dawn on the cruel beast just why Tzachok was so upset. "So...you don't like to see them like this? Well, what if I kill one of them before your very eyes? How would you like that?"

Reason was not a factor in Tza's choice; he actually hoped he might deter the end result. He dried his tears, stood up, and waited for further instructions.

"We'll take Loki first. Which one is he?"

Not often had Tza actually seen the Noor junction males, but Liam had rescued him as a young kit, and also been on the bridge when the young male had been introduced to the crew. He knew which twin wasn't Loki.

Puzzled, by the fact that Bom couldn't tell them apart, even though Loki had spent time in his prison dungeons, Tza pointed to the correct brother.

"Okay! I have something special for him. Grab his feet."

Their burden was exceedingly heavy, for Loki weighed close to six hundred pounds, but the dark tunnels they passed through were mostly downhill.

At last, the two panting males, with their load, arrived at a room that was equipped as a chamber of torture. Among the tools of torment was a miniature bared cage, bolted deep into the stone floor.

Bom unceremoniously dropped his end of the burden. The unconscious Noor's head cracked against the hard granite, resoundingly, and Tza winced in sympathy, for the headache Loki would have when he awoke.

The giant Roog/Feline swung open the small door to the four foot square, by six foot high cage.

"Put him inside," Bom ordered, pointing. "And make it quick. I'll be back shortly..."

"But...it's too small for him in there," objected Tza.

"Exactly," laughed Bom. "But you can do it. The door will lock when you shut it."

Bom was back with Liam, before Tza had accomplished his sordid task. The evil creature ignored the young male, until he had strapped the unconscious Liam to the wall in an X formation, by bands at his ankles, wrists and throat. He spun the wall, and the naked form of the second twin disappeared behind the partition.

Then, Bom came with a lock and chain, wrapped them through the bars of Loki's cage, and around the door frame, then padlocked the ends.

If ever Tza was able to bring help, he wondered how they would ever get the Noor free.

While Bom had him hauling the younger Noor, and confining them in another room, Tza racked his brain, mulling over different scenarios in which they might be set free.

The last prisoner, Liam/Loki's beautiful bride, was chained by the neck, to the stone floor of the room that contained the cage.

Then Bom lead Tza back to the shuttle.

"You are just going to leave them there?" Tza ventured. "They don't even have a light source. They'll die!"

"Oh, I'm not finished yet! I'll bring them around later," Bom declared. "First, need to deal with the shuttle. Take us back to my ship."

As they stepped from the shuttle to the metal floor of the larger ship, before Tzachok had a chance to think of fleeing, his huge antagonist grabbed him by the scruff of his neck. Suspended so, Bom litterly carried the younger Feline to his onboard transport pad.

Next thing, they were back underground again.

I am next!

Tza whined plaintively. He let go the contents of his bladder, embarrassing himself. But Bom was not the least sympathetic, only disgusted by the dribbling, dripping, whimp of a creature in his paw.

Bom roped him by the neck to a wall in a far away room, bound his paws and feet, then turned to leave the room. As he left, Tza found his bravado; he suddenly had no qualms at demanding an accounting from the devil dog/cat.

"When have I ever wronged you, Bom? What is my crime, that you sentence me to such a death of shame?"

Bom growled deep in his throat. "You served Dia, and her half Noor clan! That is offense enough in my father's world. You are nothing to me! You have served a purpose. Now, I have better things to torture...more fun than playing with you. Be thankful. You will still have a slow death by starvation."

And then he was gone, leaving Tza to deal with his fright, and regretful thoughts.

****

Across the regions of space, around the Feline seat of government, the ships just sat there. For days, by their very presence, they threatened the Feline peoples below. Then, as suddenly as they'd come, they vanished.

Shortly thereafter, the massive world was rocked by a chain reaction of subterranean explosions. The Roog had jumped demolition experts, deep into the caverns beneath the surface, where they had planted charges, set to go off, just after the Roog had left Feline space.

The shock wave from the blast that tore this vital world apart, hit the next planet in line just after noon the next day, but by then, those on it had been warned, and shields, and buffers were up.

All females from home world had been saved...all save one. With the one remaining warrior, who would not leave her side, Kei lingered behind until all were safe. Before she could step to the transporter pad behind her faithful guardian, the planet exploded.

And so at her death, began a battle like no other; for supremacy over the entire known Universe. As Kei had requested, the bearer of the original ill tidings, spread her message across the Universal battlefields, from ship to ship:

Felines are fighting for their new Sovereign! And we will find her, no matter where the Roog have taken her!

TO READ MORE GO TO AMAZON.COM